CABBAGE CATCH

Willis bounced up on the edge of the desert cabbage and rolled toward the heart of the plant.

"Don't go after him," Frank warned. "That thing might close up on you. The sun is almost down."

Willis called: "Come, Jim, boy. Warm! Stay warm all night."

"But we can't go inside a cabbage. It would crush us."

"We risk that or freezing."

The next thing they knew they were standing on the cabbage and the leaves had begun to curl around them.

"Don't talk and don't move," Frank said, "You'll use up less oxygen that way."

Jim held Willis between his legs. "What difference does it make whether we suffocate in ten minutes or an hour? Any way you figure it, we can't last till morning . . ."

"READERS YOUNG AND OLD WILL ENJOY THIS FAST-MOVING ADVENTURE NOVEL."
—*Chicago Tribune*

Red Planet

Robert A. Heinlein

A Del Rey Book

BALLANTINE BOOKS • NEW YORK

For TISH

A Del Rey Book
Published by Ballantine Books

ISBN 0-345-26069-4

This edition published by arrangement with
Charles Scribner's Sons

Manufactured in the United States of America

First Ballantine Books Edition: October 1977

CONTENTS

I

WILLIS

THE THIN AIR of Mars was chill but not really cold. It was not yet winter in southern latitudes and the daytime temperature was usually above freezing.

The queer creature standing outside the door of a dome-shaped building was generally manlike in appearance, but no human being ever had a head like that. A thing like a cox-comb jutted out above the skull, the eye lenses were wide and staring, and the front of the face stuck out in a snout. The unearthly appearance was increased by a pattern of black and yellow tiger stripes covering the entire head.

The creature was armed with a pistol-type hand weapon slung at its belt and was carrying, crooked in its right arm, a ball, larger than a basketball, smaller than a medicine ball. It moved the ball to its left arm, opened the outer door of the building and stepped inside.

Inside was a very small anteroom and an inner door. As soon as the outer door was closed the air pressure in the anteroom began to rise, accompanied by a soft sighing sound. A loudspeaker over the inner door shouted in a booming bass, "Well? Who is it? Speak up! Speak up!"

The visitor placed the ball carefully on the floor, then with both hands grasped its ugly face and pushed and lifted it to the top of its head. Underneath was disclosed the face of an Earth-human boy. "It's Jim Marlowe, Doc," he answered.

"Well, come in. Come in! Don't stand out there chewing your nails."

"Coming." When the air pressure in the anteroom had equalized with the pressure in the rest of the house the inner door opened automatically. Jim said, "Come along, Willis," and went on in.

The ball developed three spaced bumps on its lower side and followed after him, in a gait which combined spinning, walking, and rolling. More correctly, it careened, like a barrel being manhandled along a dock. They went down a passage and entered a large room that occupied half the floorspace of the circular house plan. Doctor MacRae looked up but did not get up. "Howdy, Jim. Skin yourself. Coffee on the bench. Howdy, Willis," he added and turned back to his work. He was dressing the hand of a boy about Jim's age.

"Thanks, Doc. Oh—hello, Francis. What are you doing here?"

"Hi, Jim. I killed a water-seeker, then I cut my thumb on one of its spines."

"Quit squirming!" commanded the doctor.

"That stuff stings," protested Francis.

"I meant it to."

"How in the world did you do that?" persisted Jim. "You ought to know better than to touch one of those things. Just burn 'em down and burn 'em up." He zipped open the front of his outdoor costume, peeled it off his arms and legs and hung it on a rack near the door. The rack held Francis' suit, the headpiece of which was painted in bright colors like an Indian brave's war paint, and the doctor's suit, the mask of which was plain. Jim was now stylishly and appropriately dressed for indoors on Mars—in bright red shorts.

"I did burn it," explained Francis, "but it moved when I touched it. I wanted to get the tail to make a necklace."

"Then you didn't burn it right. Probably left it full of live eggs. Who're you making a necklace for?"

"None of your business. And I did so burn the egg sac. What do you take me for? A tourist?"

"Sometimes I wonder. You know those things don't die until sundown."

"Don't talk nonsense, Jim," the doctor advised. "Now,

Frank, I'm going to give you an antitoxin shot. 'Twon't do you any good but it'll make your mother happy. Long about tomorrow your thumb will swell up like a poisoned pup; bring it back and I'll lance it."

"Am I going to lose my thumb?" the boy asked.

"No. But you'll do your scratching with your left hand for a few days. Now, Jim, what brings you here? Tummyache?"

"No, Doc. It's Willis."

"Willis, eh? He looks pert enough to me." The doctor stared down at the creature. Willis was at his feet, having come up to watch the dressing of Frank's thumb. To do so he had protruded three eye stalks from the top of his spherical mass. The stalks stuck up like thumbs, in an equal-sided triangle, and from each popped a disturbingly human eye. The little fellow turned around slowly on his tripod of bumps, or pseudopeds, and gave each of his eyes a chance to examine the doctor.

"Get me a cup of Java, Jim," commanded the doctor, then leaned over and made a cradle of his hands. "Here, Willis, upsi-daisy!" Willis gave a little bounce and landed in the doctor's hands, withdrawing all protuberances as he did so. The doctor lifted him to the examining table; Willis promptly stuck out legs and eyes again. They stared at each other.

The doctor saw a ball covered with thick, close-cropped fur, like sheared sheepskin, and featureless at the moment save for supports and eye stalks. The Mars creature saw an elderly male Earthman almost completely covered with wiry grey-and-white hair. The middle portion of this strange, un-Martian creature was concealed in snow-white shorts and shirt. Willis enjoyed looking at him.

"How do you feel, Willis?" inquired the doctor. "Feel good? Feel bad?"

A dimple showed at the very crown of the ball between the stalks, dilated to an opening. "Willis fine!" he said. His voice was remarkably like Jim's.

"Fine, eh?" Without looking around the doctor added, "Jim! Wash those cups again. And this time, sterilize them. Want everybody around here to come down with the pip?"

"Okay, Doc," Jim acknowledged, and added to Francis, "You want some coffee, too?"

"Sure. Weak, with plenty of cow."

"Don't be fussy." Jim dipped into the laboratory sink and managed to snag another cup. The sink was filled with dirty dishes. Nearby a large flask of coffee simmered over a Bunsen burner. Jim washed three cups carefully, put them through the sterilizer, then filled them.

Doctor MacRae accepted a cup and said, "Jim, this citizen says he's okay. What's the trouble?"

"I know he says he's all right, Doc, but he's not. Can't you examine him and find out?"

"Examine him? How, boy? I can't even take his temperature because I don't know what his temperature ought to be. I know as much about his body chemistry as a pig knows about pattycake. Want me to cut him open and see what makes him tick?"

Willis promptly withdrew all projections and became as featureless as a billiard ball. "Now you've scared him," Jim said accusingly.

"Sorry." The doctor reached out and commenced scratching and tickling the furry ball. "Good Willis, nice Willis. Nobody's going to hurt Willis. Come on, boy, come out of your hole."

Willis barely dilated the sphincter over his speaking diaphragm. "Not hurt Willis?" he said anxiously in Jim's voice.

"Not hurt Willis. Promise."

"Not cut Willis?"

"Not cut Willis. Not a bit."

The eyes poked out slowly. Somehow he managed an expression of watchful caution, though he had nothing resembling a face. "That's better," said the doctor. "Let's get to the point, Jim. What makes you think there's something wrong with this fellow, when he and I can't see it?"

"Well, Doc, it's the way he behaves. He's all right indoors, but outdoors— He used to follow me everywhere, bouncing around the landscape, poking his nose into everything."

"He hasn't got a nose," Francis commented.

"Go to the head of the class. But now, when I take him out, he just goes into a ball and I can't get a thing out of him. If he's not sick, why does he act that way?"

"I begin to get a glimmering," Doctor MacRae answered. "How long have you been teamed up with this balloon?"

Jim thought back over the twenty-four months of the Martian year. "Since along toward the end of Zeus, nearly November."

"And now here it is the last of March, almost Ceres, and the summer gone. That suggest anything to your mind?"

"Uh, no."

"You expect him to go hopping around through the snow? We migrate when it gets cold; he lives here."

Jim's mouth dropped open. "You mean he's trying to hibernate?"

"What else? Willis's ancestors have had a good many millions of years to get used to the seasons around here; you can't expect him to ignore them."

Jim looked worried. "I had planned to take him with me to Syrtis Minor."

"Syrtis Minor? Oh, yes, you go away to school this year, don't you? You, too, Frank."

"You bet!"

"I can't get used to the way you kids grow up. I came to Mars so that the years would be twice as long, but it doesn't seem to make any difference—they spin faster."

"Say, Doc, how old are you?" inquired Francis.

"Never mind. Which one of you is going to study medicine and come back to help me with my practice?"

Neither one answered. "Speak up, speak up!" urged the doctor. "What are you going to study?"

Jim said, "Well, I don't know. I'm interested in areography,* but I like biology, too. Maybe I'll be a planetary economist, like my old man."

"That's a big subject. Ought to keep you busy a long time. You, Frank?"

* Areography: equivalent to "geography" for Earth. From "Ares," Greek for Mars.

Francis looked slightly embarrassed. "Well, uh—shucks, I think I'd like to be a rocket pilot."

"I thought you had outgrown that."

"Why not?" Francis answered. "I might make it."

"On your own head be it. Speaking of such things, you younkers go to school before the colony migrates, don't you?" Since Earth-humans do not hibernate, it was necessary that the colony migrate twice each Martian year. The southern summer was spent at Charax, only thirty degrees from the southern pole; the colony was now about to move to Copais in Utopia, almost as far to the north, there to remain half a Martian year, or almost a full Earth year.

There were year-around establishments near the equator—New Shanghai, Marsport, Syrtis Minor, others—but they were not truly colonies, being manned mainly by employees of the Mars Company. By contract and by charter the Company was required to provide advanced terrestrial education on Mars for colonials; it suited the Company to provide it only at Syrtis Minor.

"We go next Wednesday," said Jim, "on the mail scooter."

"So soon?"

"Yes, and that's what worries me about Willis. What ought I to do, Doc?"

Willis heard his name and looked inquiringly at Jim. He repeated, in exact imitation of Jim, " 'What ought I to do, Doc?' "

"Shut up, Willis——"

" 'Shut up, Willis.' " Willis imitated the doctor just as perfectly.

"Probably the kindest thing would be to take him out, find him a hole, and stuff him in it. You can renew your acquaintance when he's through hibernating."

"But, Doc, that means I'll lose him! He'll be out long before I'm home from school. Why, he'll probably wake up even before the colony comes back."

"Probably." MacRae thought about it. "It won't hurt him to be on his own again. It's not a natural life he leads with you, Jim. He's an individual, you know; he's not property."

"Of course he's not! He's my friend."

"I can't see," put in Francis, "why Jim sets such store by him. Sure, he talks a lot, but most of it is just parrot stuff. He's a moron, if you ask me."

"Nobody asked you. Willis is fond of me, aren't you, Willis? Here, come to papa." Jim spread his arms; the little Martian creature hopped into them and settled in his lap, a warm, furry mass, faintly pulsating. Jim stroked him.

"Why don't you ask one of the Martians?" suggested MacRae.

"I tried to, but I couldn't find one that was in a mood to pay any attention."

"You mean you weren't willing to wait long enough. A Martian will notice you if you're patient. Well, why don't you ask *him*? He can speak for himself."

"What should I say?"

"I'll try it. Willis!"

Willis turned two eyes on the doctor; MacRae went on, "Want to go outdoors and find a place to sleep?"

"Willis not sleepy."

"Get sleepy outdoors. Nice and cold, find hole in ground. Curl up and take good long sleep. How about it?"

"No!" The doctor had to look sharply to see that it was not Jim who had answered; when Willis spoke for himself he always used Jim's voice. Willis's sound diaphragm had no special quality of its own, any more than has the diaphragm of a radio loudspeaker. It was much like a loudspeaker's diaphragm, save that it was part of a living animal.

"That seems definite, but we'll try it from another angle. Willis, do you want to stay with Jim?"

"Willis stay with Jim." Willis added meditatively, "Warm!"

"There's the key to your charm, Jim," the doctor said dryly. "He likes your blood temperature. But *ipse dixit*—keep him with you. I don't think it will hurt him. He may live fifty years instead of a hundred, but he'll have twice as much fun."

"Do they normally live to be a hundred?" asked Jim.

"Who knows? We haven't been around this planet long enough to know such things. Now come on, get out. I've got work to do." The doctor eyed his bed thoughtfully. It had not been made in a week; he decided to let it wait until wash day.

"What does '*ipse dixit*' mean, Doc?" asked Francis.

"It means, 'He sure said a mouthful.' "

"Doc," suggested Jim, "why don't you have dinner with us tonight? I'll call mother. You, too, Frank."

"Not me," Frank said. "I'd better not. My mother says I eat too many meals with you folks."

"My mother, if she were here, would undoubtedly say the same thing," admitted the doctor. "Call your mother, Jim."

Jim went to the phone, tuned out two colonial housewives gossiping about babies, and finally reached his home on an alternate frequency. When his mother's face appeared on the screen he explained his wish. "Delighted to have the doctor with us," she said. "Tell him to hurry along, Jimmy."

"Right away, Mom!" Jim switched off and reached for his outdoor suit.

"Don't put it on," advised MacRae. "It's too chilly out. We'll go through the tunnels."

"It's twice as far," objected Jim.

"We'll leave it up to Willis. Willis, how do you vote?"

"Warm," said Willis smugly.

II

SOUTH COLONY, MARS

South Colony was arranged like a wheel. The administration building was the hub; tunnels ran out in all directions and buildings were placed over them. A rim tunnel had been started to join the spokes at the edge of the wheel; thus far a forty-five degree arc had been completed.

Save for three Moon huts erected when the colony was founded and since abandoned, all the buildings were shaped alike. Each was a hemispherical bubble of silicone plastic, processed from the soil of Mars and blown on the spot. Each was a double bubble, in fact; first one large bubble would be blown, say thirty or forty feet across; when it had hardened, the new building would be entered through the tunnel and an inner bubble, slightly smaller than the first, would be blown. The outer bubble "polymerized"—that is to say, cured and hardened, under the rays of the sun; a battery of ultra-violet and heat lamps cured the inner. The walls were separated by a foot of dead air space, which provided insulation against the bitter sub-zero nights of Mars.

When a new building had hardened, a door would be cut to the outside and a pressure lock installed; the colonials maintained about two-thirds Earth-normal pressure indoors for comfort and the pressure on Mars is never as much as half of that. A visitor from Earth, not conditioned to the planet, will die without a respirator. Among the colonists only Tibetans and Bolivian Indians will venture outdoors without respirators and even they will wear the snug elastic Mars suit to avoid skin hemorrhages.

Buildings had not even view windows, any more than a modern building in New York has. The surrounding desert, while beautiful, is monotonous. South Colony was in an area granted by the Martians, just north of the ancient city of Charax—there is no need to give the Martian name since an Earthman can't pronounce it—and between the legs of the double canal Strymon. Again we follow colonial custom in using the name assigned by the immortal Dr. Percival Lowell.

Francis accompanied Jim and Doctor MacRae as far as the junction of the tunnels under city hall, then turned down his own tunnel. A few minutes later the doctor and Jim—and Willis—ascended into the Marlowe home. Jim's mother met them; Doctor MacRae bowed. "Madame, I am again imposing on your good nature."

"Fiddlesticks, Doctor. You are always welcome at our table."

"I would that I had the character to wish that you were not so superlative a cook, that you might know the certain truth: it is yourself, my dear, that brings me here."

Jim's mother blushed. She changed the subject, "Jim, hang up your pistol. Don't leave it on the sofa where Oliver can get it."

Jim's baby brother, hearing his name, immediately made a dash for the pistol. Jim and his sister Phyllis both saw this, both yelled, "Ollie!"—and were immediately mimicked by Willis, who performed the difficult trick, possible only to an atonal diaphragm, of duplicating both voices simultaneously.

Phyllis was nearer; she grabbed the gun and slapped the child's hands. Oliver began to cry, reinforced by Willis. "Children!" said Mrs. Marlowe, just as Mr. Marlowe appeared in the door.

"What's all the ruckus?" he inquired mildly.

Doctor MacRae picked up Oliver, turned him upside down, and sat him on his shoulders. Oliver forgot that he was crying. Mrs. Marlowe turned to her husband. "Nothing, darling. I'm glad you're home. Children, go wash for dinner, all of you.

The second generation trooped out. "What was the trouble?" Mr. Marlowe repeated.

A few moments later Mr. Marlowe joined Jim in his son's room. "Jim?"

"Yes, Dad."

"What's this about your leaving your gun where the baby could reach it?"

Jim flushed. "It wasn't charged, Dad."

"If all the people who had been killed with unloaded guns were laid end to end it would make quite a line up. You are proud of being a licensed gun wearer, aren't you?"

"Uh, yes, sir."

"And I'm proud to have you be one. It means you are a responsible, trusted adult. But when I sponsored you before the Council and stood up with you when you took your oath, I guaranteed that you would obey the regulations and follow the code, wholeheartedly and all the time—not just most of the time. Understand me?"

"Yes, sir. I think I do."

"Good. Let's go in to dinner."

Doctor MacRae dominated the dinnertable talk, as he always did, with a soft rumble of salty comments and outrageous observations. Presently he turned to Mr. Marlowe and said, "You said something earlier about another twenty years and we could throw away our respirators; tell me: is there news about the Project?"

The colony had dozens of projects, all intended to make Mars more livable for human beings, but *the* Project always meant the atmosphere, or oxygen, project. The pioneers of the Harvard-Carnegie expedition reported Mars suitable for colonization except for the all-important fact that the air was so thin that a normal man would suffocate. However they reported also that many, many billions of tons of oxygen were locked in the Martian desert sands, the red iron oxides that give Mars its ruddy color. The Project proposed to free this oxygen for humans to breathe.

"Didn't you hear the Deimos newscast this afternoon?" Mr. Marlowe answered.

"Never listen to newscasts. Saves wear and tear on the nervous system."

"No doubt. But this was good news. The pilot plant in Libya is in operation, successful operation. The first day's run restored nearly four million tons mass of oxygen to the air—and no breakdowns."

Mrs. Marlowe looked startled. "Four million tons? That seems a tremendous lot."

Her husband grinned. "Any idea how long it would take that one plant at that rate to do the job, that is, increase the oxygen pressure by five mass-pounds per square inch?"

"Of course I haven't. But not very long I should think."

"Let me see—" His lips moved soundlessly. "Uh, around two hundred thousand years—Mars years, of course."

"James, you're teasing me!"

"No, I'm not. Don't let big figures frighten you, my dear; of course we won't depend on one plant; they'll be scattered every fifty miles or so through the desert, a thousand mega-horsepower each. There's no limit to the power avail-

17

able, thank goodness; if we don't clean up the job in our lifetimes, at least the kids will certainly see the end of it."

Mrs. Marlowe looked dreamy. "That would be nice, to walk outside with your bare face in the breeze. I remember when I was a little girl, we had an orchard with a stream running through it—" She stopped.

"Sorry we came to Mars, Jane?" her husband asked softly.

"Oh, no! This is my home."

"Good. What are you looking sour about, Doctor?"

"Eh? Oh, nothing, nothing! I was just thinking about the end result. Mind you, this is fine work, all of it—hard work, good work, that a man can get his teeth into. But we get it done and what for? So that another two billion, three billion sheep can fiddle around with nonsense, spend their time scratching themselves and *baa*ing. We should have left Mars to the Martians. Tell me, sir, do you know what television was used for when it first came out?"

"No. How would I?"

"Well, I didn't see it myself of course, but my father told me about it. It seems——"

"Your *father*? How old was he? When was he born?"

"My grandfather, then. Or it may have been my great grandfather. That's beside the point. They installed the first television sets in cocktail bars—amusement places—and used to watch wrestling matches."

"What's a 'wrestling match'?" demanded Phyllis.

"An obsolete form of folk dancing," explained her father. "Never mind. Granting your point, Doctor, I see no harm——"

"What's 'folk dancing'?" persisted Phyllis.

"You tell her, Jane. She's got me stumped."

Jim looked smug. "It's when folks dance, silly."

"That's near enough," agreed his mother.

Doctor MacRae stared. "These kids are missing something. I think I'll organize a square dancing club. I used to be a pretty good caller, once upon a time."

Phyllis turned to her brother. "Now I suppose you'll tell me that square dancing is when a square dances."

Mr. Marlowe raised his eyebrows. "I think the children have all finished, my dear. Couldn't they be excused?"

"Yes, surely. You may leave, my dears. Say 'Excuse me, please,' Ollie." The baby repeated it, with Willis in mirror chorus.

Jim hastily wiped his mouth, grabbed Willis, and headed for his own room. He liked to hear the doctor talk but he had to admit that the old boy could babble the most fantastic nonsense when other grown-ups were around. Nor did the discussion of the oxygen project interest Jim; he saw nothing strange nor uncomfortable about wearing his mask. He would feel undressed going outdoors without it.

From Jim's point of view Mars was all right the way it was, no need to try to make it more like Earth. Earth was no great shakes anyway. His own personal recollection of Earth was limited to vague memories from early childhood of the emigrants' conditioning station on the high Bolivian plateau—cold, shortness of breath, and great weariness.

His sister trailed after him. He stopped just inside his door and said, "What do you want, shorty?"

"Well. . . . Lookie, Jimmy, seeing as I'm going to have to take care of Willis after you've gone away to school, maybe it would be a good idea for you to sort of explain it to him, so he would do what I tell him without any trouble."

Jim stared. "Whatever gave you the notion I was going to leave him behind?"

She stared back. "But you are! You'll *have* to. You can't take him to school. You ask mother."

"Mother hasn't anything to do with it. She doesn't care what I take to school."

"Well, you oughtn't to take him, even if she doesn't object. I think you're mean."

"You always think I'm mean if I don't cater to your every wish!"

"Not to me—to Willis. This is Willis's home; he's used to it. He'll be homesick away at school."

"He'll have me!"

"Not most of the time, he won't. You'll be in class. Willis wouldn't have anything to do but sit and mope. You ought to leave him here with me—with us—where he'd be happy."

Jim straightened himself up. "I'm going to find out about

19

this, right away." He walked back into the living compartment and waited aggressively to be noticed. Shortly his father turned toward him.

"Yes? What is it, Jim? Something eating you?"

"Uh, well—look, Dad, is there any doubt about Willis going with me when I go away to school?"

His father looked surprised. "It had never occurred to me that you would consider taking him."

"Huh? Why not?"

"Well, school is hardly the place for him."

"Why?"

"Well, you wouldn't be able to take care of him properly. You'll be awfully busy."

"Willis doesn't take much care. Just feed him every month or so and give him a drink about once a week and he doesn't ask for anything else. Why can't I take him, Dad?"

Mr. Marlowe looked baffled; he turned to his wife. She started in, "Now, Jimmy darling, we don't want you to——"

Jim interrupted, "Mother, every time you want to talk me out of something you start out, 'Jimmy darling'!"

Her mouth twitched but she kept from smiling. "Sorry, Jim. Perhaps I do. What I was trying to say was this: we want you to get off to a good start at school. I don't believe that having Willis on your hands will help any."

Jim was stumped for the moment, but was not ready to give up. "Look, Mother. Look, Dad. You both saw the pamphlet the school sent me, telling me what to do and what to bring and when to show up and so forth. If either one of you can find anything anywhere in those instructions that says I can't take Willis with me, I'll shut up like a Martian. Is that fair?"

Mrs. Marlowe looked inquiringly at her husband. He looked back at her with the same appeal for help in his expression. He was acutely aware that Doctor MacRae was watching both of them, not saying a word but wearing an expression of sardonic amusement.

Mr. Marlowe shrugged. "Take Willis along, Jim. But he's your problem."

Jim's face broke out in a grin. "Thanks, Dad!" He left the

room quickly in order not to give his parents time to change their minds.

Mr. Marlowe banged his pipe on an ashtray and glowered at Doctor MacRae. "Well, what are you grinning at, you ancient ape? You think I'm too indulgent, don't you?"

"Oh, no, not at all! I think you did perfectly right."

"You think that pet of Jim's won't cause him trouble at school?"

"On the contrary. I have some familiarity with Willis's peculiar social habits."

"Then why do you say I did right?"

"Why shouldn't the boy have trouble? Trouble is the normal condition for the human race. We were raised on it. We thrive on it."

"Sometimes, Doctor, I think that you are, as Jim would put it, crazy as a spin bug."

"Probably. But since I am the only medical man around, I am not likely to be committed for it. Mrs. Marlowe, could you favor an old man with another cup of your delicious coffee?"

"Certainly, Doctor." She poured for him, then went on. "James, I am not sorry you decided to let Jim take Willis. It will be a relief."

"Why, dear? Jim was correct when he said that the little beggar isn't much trouble."

"Well, he isn't really. But—I just wish he weren't so truthful."

"So? I thought he was the perfect witness in settling the children's squabbles?"

"Oh, he is. He'll play back anything he hears as accurately as a transcriber. That's the trouble." She looked upset, then chuckled. "You know Mrs. Pottle?"

"Of course."

The doctor added, "How can one avoid it? I, unhappy man, am in charge of her 'nerves'."

Mrs. Marlowe asked, "Is she actually sick, Doctor?"

"She eats too much and doesn't work enough. Further communication is forbidden by professional ethics."

"I didn't know you had any."

"Young lady, show respect for my white hairs. What about this Pottle female?"

"Well, Luba Konski had lunch with me last week and we got to talking about Mrs. Pottle. Honest, James, I didn't say much and I did not know that Willis was under the table."

"He was?" Mr. Marlowe covered his eyes. "Do go on."

"Well, you both remember that the Konskis housed the Pottles at North Colony until a house was built for them. Sarah Pottle has been Luba's pet hate ever since, and Tuesday Luba was giving me some juicy details on Sarah's habits at home. Two days later Sarah Pottle stopped by to give me advice on how to bring up children. Something she said triggered Willis—I knew he was in the room but I didn't think anything of it—and Willis put on just the wrong record and I couldn't shut him up. I finally carried him out of the room. Mrs. Pottle left without saying goodbye and I haven't heard from her since."

"That's no loss," her husband commented.

"True, but it got Luba in Dutch. No one could miss Luba's accent and Willis does it better than she does herself. I don't think Luba minds, though—and you should have heard Willis's playback of Luba's description of how Sarah Pottle looks in the morning—and what she does about it."

"You should hear," answered MacRae, "Mrs. Pottle's opinions on the servant problem."

"I have. She thinks it's a scandal that the Company doesn't import servants for us."

The doctor nodded. "With collars riveted around their necks."

"That woman! I can't see why she ever became a colonist."

"Didn't you know?" her husband said. "They came out here expecting to get rich in a hurry."

"Hummph!"

Doctor MacRae got a far-away look. "Mrs. Marlowe, speaking as her physician, it might help me to hear what Willis has to say about Mrs. Pottle. Do you suppose he would recite for us?"

"Doctor, you're an old fraud, with a taste for gossip."

"Granted. I like also eavesdropping."

"You're shameless."

"Again granted. My nerves are relaxed. I haven't felt ashamed in years."

"Willis may just give a thrilling account of the children's chit-chat for the past two weeks."

"Perhaps if you coaxed him?"

Mrs. Marlowe suddenly dimpled. "It won't hurt to try." She left the room to fetch Jim's globular friend.

III

GEKKO

WEDNESDAY MORNING dawned clear and cold, as mornings have a habit of doing on Mars. The Suttons and the Marlowes, minus Oliver, were gathered at the Colony's cargo dock on the west leg of Strymon canal, ready to see the boys off.

The temperature was rising and the dawn wind was blowing firmly, but it was still at least thirty below. Strymon canal was a steel-blue, hard sheet of ice and would not melt today in this latitude. Resting on it beside the dock was the mail scooter from Syrtis Minor, its boat body supported by razor-edged runners. The driver was still loading it with cargo dragged from the warehouse on the dock.

The tiger stripes on Jim's mask, the war paint on Frank's, and a rainbow motif on Phyllis's made the young people easy to identify. The adults could be told apart only by size, shape, and manner; there were two extras, Doctor MacRae and Father Cleary. The priest was talking in low, earnest tones to Frank.

He turned presently and spoke to Jim. "Your own pastor

asked me to say good-by to you, son. Unfortunately the poor man is laid up with a touch of Mars throat. He would have come anyhow had I not hidden his mask." The Protestant chaplain, as well as the priest, was a bachelor; the two shared a house.

"Is he very sick?" asked Jim.

"Not that sick. But take his blessing—and mine too." He offered his hand.

Jim dropped his travel bag, shifted his ice skates and Willis over to his left arm and shook hands. There followed an awkward silence. Finally Jim said, "Why don't you all go inside before you freeze to death?"

"Yeah," agreed Francis. "That's a good idea."

"I think the driver is about ready now," Mr. Marlowe countered. "Well, son, take care of yourself. We'll see you at migration." He shook hands solemnly.

"So long, Dad."

Mrs. Marlowe put her arms around him, pressed her mask against his and said, "Oh, my little boy—you're too young to go away from home!"

"Oh, Mother, please!" But he hugged her. Then Phyllis had to be hugged. The driver called out:

" 'Board!' "

" 'Bye everybody!" Jim turned away, felt his elbow caught. It was the doctor. "Take care of yourself, Jim. And don't take any guff off of anybody."

"Thanks, Doc." Jim turned and presented his school authorization to the driver while the doctor bade Francis good-by.

The driver looked it over. "Both deadheads, eh? Well, seeing as how there aren't any pay passengers this morning you can ride in the observatory." He tore off his copy; Jim climbed inside and went up to the prized observation seats behind and above the driver's compartment. Frank joined him.

The craft trembled as the driver jacked the runners loose from the ice, then with a roar from the turbine and a soft, easy surge the car got under way. The banks flowed past them and melted into featureless walls as the speed picked up. The ice was mirror smooth; they soon reached cruising speed of better than two hundred fifty miles per hour. Presently the driver removed his mask; Jim and Frank, seeing him, did likewise. The car was pressurized now by an air ram faced into their own wind of motion; it was much warmer, too, from the air's compression.

"Isn't this swell?" said Francis.

"Yes. Look at Earth."

Their mother planet was riding high above the Sun in the northeastern sky. It blazed green against a deep purple background. Close to it, but easy to separate with the naked eye, was a lesser, pure white star—Luna, Earth's moon. Due north of them, in the direction they were going, Deimos, Mars' outer moon, hung no more than twenty degrees above the horizon. Almost lost in the rays of the sun, it was a tiny pale disc, hardly more than a dim star and much outshone by Earth.

Phobos, the inner moon, was not in sight. At the latitude of Charax it never rose more than eight degrees or so above the northern horizon and that for an hour or less, twice a day. In the daytime it was lost in the blue of the horizon and no one would be so foolhardy as to watch for it in the bitter night. Jim did not remember ever having seen it except during migration between colonies.

Francis looked from Earth to Deimos. "Ask the driver to turn on the radio," he suggested. "Deimos is up."

"Who cares about the broadcast?" Jim answered. "I want to watch." The banks were not so high now; from the observation dome he could see over them into the fields beyond. Although it was late in the season the irrigated belt near the canal was still green and getting greener as he watched, as the plants came out of the ground to seek the morning sunlight.

He could make out, miles away, an occasional ruddy sand dune of the open desert. He could not see the green belt of the east leg of their canal; it was over the horizon.

Without urging, the driver switched on his radio; music filled the car and blotted out the monotonous low roar of the turbo-jet. It was terrestrial music, by Sibelius, a classical composer of another century. Mars colony had not yet found time to develop its own arts and still borrowed its culture. But neither Jim nor Frank knew who the composer was, nor cared. The banks of the canal had closed in again; there was nothing to see but the straight ribbon of ice; they settled back and daydreamed.

Willis stirred for the first time since he had struck the outer cold. He extended his eye stalks, looked inquiringly around, then commenced to beat time with them.

Presently the music stopped and a voice said: "This is station D-M-S, the Mars Company, Deimos, *circum* Mars. We bring you now by relay from Syrtis Minor a program in the public interest. Doctor Graves Armbruster will speak on 'Ecological Considerations involved in Experimental Artificial Symbiotics as related to——' "

The driver promptly switched the radio off.

"I would like to have heard that," objected Jim. "It sounded interesting."

"Oh, you're just showing off," Frank answered. "You don't even know what those words mean."

"The dickens I don't. It means——"

"Shut up and take a nap." Taking his own advice Frank lay back and closed his eyes. However he got no chance to sleep. Willis had apparently been chewing over, in whatever it was he used for a mind, the program he had just heard. He opened up and started to play it back, woodwinds and all.

The driver looked back and up, looked startled. He said something but Willis drowned him out. Willis bulled on through to the end, even to the broken-off announcement. The driver finally made himself heard. "Hey, you guys! What you got up there? A portable recorder?"

"No, a bouncer."

"A what?"

Jim held Willis up so that the driver could see him. "A bouncer. His name is Willis." The driver stared.

"You mean *that* thing is a recorder?"

"No, he's a bouncer. As I said, his name is Willis."

"This I got to see," announced the driver. He did something at his control board, then turned around and stuck his head and shoulders up into the observation dome.

Frank said, "Hey! You'll wreck us."

"Relax," advised the driver. "I put her on echo-automatic. High banks for the next couple o' hundred miles. Now what is this gismo? When you brought it aboard I thought it was a volley ball."

"No, it's Willis. Say hello to the man, Willis."

"Hello, man," Willis answered agreeably.

The driver scratched his head. "This beats anything I ever saw in Keokuk. Sort of a parrot, eh?"

"He's a bouncer. He's got a scientific name, but it just means 'Martian roundhead'. Never seen one before?"

"No. You know, bud, this is the screwiest planet in the whole system."

"If you don't like it here," asked Jim, "why don't you go back where you came from?"

"Don't go popping off, youngster. How much will you take for the gismo? I got an idea I could use him."

"Sell Willis? Are you crazy?"

"Sometimes I think so. Oh, well, it was just an idea." The driver went back to his station, stopping once to look back and stare at Willis.

The boys dug sandwiches out of their travel bags and munched them. After that Frank's notion about a nap seemed a good idea. They slept until wakened by the car slowing down. Jim sat up, blinked, and called down, "What's up?"

"Coming into Cynia Station," the driver answered. "Lay over until sundown."

"Won't the ice hold?"

"Maybe it will. Maybe it won't. The temperature's up and I'm not going to chance it." The car slid softly to a stop then started again and crawled slowly up a low ramp, stopped again. "All out!" the driver called. "Be back by sundown—or get left." He climbed out; the boys followed.

Cynia Station was three miles west of the ancient city of Cynia, where west Strymon joins the canal Oeroe. It was merely a lunchroom, a bunkhouse, and a row of pre-fab warehouses. To the east the feathery towers of Cynia gleamed in the sky, seemed almost to float, too beautifully unreal to be solid.

The driver went into the little inn. Jim wanted to walk over and explore the city; Frank favored stopping in the restaurant first. Frank won out. They went inside and cautiously invested part of their meager capital in coffee and some indifferent soup.

The driver looked up from his dinner presently and said, "Hey, George! Ever see anything like that?" He pointed to Willis.

George was the waiter. He was also the cashier, the hotel keeper, the station agent, and the Company representative. He glanced at Willis. "Yep."

"You did, huh? Where? Do you suppose I could find one?"

"Doubt it. You see 'em sometimes, hanging around the Martians. Not many of 'em." He turned back to his reading—a New York *Times*, more than two years old.

The boys finished, paid their bills, and prepared to go outside. The cook-waiter-station-agent said, "Hold on. Where are you kids going?"

"Syrtis Minor."

"Not that. Where are you going right now? Why don't you wait in the dormitory? Take a nap if you like."

"We thought we would kind of explore around outside," explained Jim.

"Okay. But stay away from the city."

"Why?"

"Because the Company doesn't allow it, that's why. Not without permission. So stay clear of it."

"How do we get permission?" Jim persisted.

"You can't. Cynia hasn't been opened up to exploitation yet." He went back to his reading.

Jim was about to continue the matter but Frank tugged at his sleeve. They went outside together. Jim said, "I don't think he has any business telling us we can't go to Cynia."

"What's the difference? He thinks he has."

"What'll we do now?"

"Go to Cynia, of course. Only we won't consult his nibs."

"Suppose he catches us?"

"How can he? He won't stir off that stool he's warming. Come on."

"Okay." They set out to the east. The going was not too easy; there was no road of any sort and all the plant growth bordering the canal was spread out to its greatest extent to catch the rays of the midday sun. But Mars' low gravity makes walking easy work even over rough ground. They came shortly to the bank of Oeroe and followed it to the right, toward the city.

The way was easy along the smooth stone of the bank. The air was warm and balmy even though the surface of the canal was still partly frozen. The sun was high; they were the better part of a thousand miles closer to the equator than they had been at daybreak.

"Warm," said Willis. "Willis want down."

"Okay," Jim agreed, "but don't fall in."

"Willis not fall in." Jim put him down and the little creature went skipping and rolling along the bank, with occasional excursions into the thick vegetation, like a puppy exploring a new pasture.

They had gone perhaps a mile and the towers of the city were higher in the sky when they encountered a Martian. He was a small specimen of his sort, being not over twelve feet tall. He was standing quite still, all three of his legs down, apparently lost in contemplation of the whichness of what. The eye facing them stared unblinkingly.

Jim and Frank were, of course, used to Martians and recognized that this one was busy in his "other world"; they stopped talking and continued on past him, being careful not to brush against his legs.

Not so Willis. He went darting around the Martian's peds, rubbing against them, then stopped and let out a couple of mournful croaks.

The Martian stirred, looking around him, and suddenly bent and scooped Willis up.

"Hey!" yelled Jim. "Put him down!"

No answer.

Jim turned hastily to Frank. "You talk to him, Frank.

I'll never be able to make him understand me. Please!" Of the Martian dominant language Jim understood little and spoke less. Frank was somewhat better, but only by comparison. Those who speak Martian complain that it hurts their throats.

"What'll I say?"

"Tell him to put Willis down!"

"Relax. Martians never hurt anybody."

"Well, tell him to put Willis down, then."

"I'll try." Frank screwed up his mouth and got to work. His accent, bad at best, was made worse by the respirator and by nervousness. Nevertheless he clucked and croaked his way through a phrase that seemed to mean what Jim wanted. Nothing happened.

He tried again, using a different idiom; still nothing happened. "It's no good, Jim," he admitted. "Either he doesn't understand me or he doesn't want to bother to listen."

Jim shouted, "Willis! Hey, Willis! Are you all right?"

"Willis fine!"

"Jump down! I'll catch you."

"Willis fine."

The Martian wobbled his head, seemed to locate Jim for the first time. He cradled Willis in one arm; his other two arms came snaking suddenly down and enclosed Jim, one palm flap cradling him where he sat down, the other slapping him across the belly.

He felt himself lifted and held and then he was staring into a large liquid Martian eye which stared back at him. The Martian "man" rocked his head back and forth and let each of his eyes have a good look.

It was the closest Jim had ever been to a Martian; he did not care for it. Jim tried to wiggle away, but the fragile-appearing Martian was stronger than he was.

Suddenly the Martian's voice boomed out from the top of his head. Jim could not understand what was being said although he spotted the question symbol at the beginning of the phrase. But the Martian's voice had a strange effect on him. Croaking and uncouth though it was, it was filled with such warmth and sympathy and friendliness that the native no longer frightened him. Instead he seemed like an old and trusted friend.

The Martian repeated the question.

"What did he say, Frank?"

"I didn't get it. He's friendly but I can't understand him."

The Martian spoke again; Frank listened. "He's inviting you to go with him, I think."

Jim hesitated a split second. "Tell him okay."

"Jim, are you crazy?"

"It's all right. He means well. I'm sure of it."

"Well—all right." Frank croaked the phrase of assent.

The native gathered up one leg and strode rapidly away toward the city. Frank trotted after. He tried his best to keep up, but the pace was too much for him. He paused, gasping, then shouted, "Wait for me," his voice muffled by his mask.

Jim tried to phrase a demand to stop, gave up, then got an inspiration. "Say, Willis—Willis boy. Tell him to wait for Frank."

"Wait for Frank?" Willis said doubtfully.

"Yes. Wait for Frank."

"Okay." Willis hooted at his new friend; the Martian paused and dropped his third leg. Frank came puffing up.

The Martian removed one arm from Jim and scooped up Frank with it. "Hey!" Frank protested. "Cut it out."

"Take it easy," advised Jim.

"But I don't want to be carried."

Frank's reply was disturbed by the Martian starting up again. Thus burdened, he shifted to a three-legged gait in which at least two legs were always on the ground. It was bumpy but surprisingly fast.

"Where do you suppose he is taking us?" asked Jim.

"To the city I guess." Frank added, "We don't want to miss the scooter."

"We've got hours yet. Quit worrying."

The Martian said nothing more but continued slogging toward Cynia. Willis was evidently as happy as a bee in a flower shop. Jim settled down to enjoying the ride. Now that he was being carried with his head a good ten feet above ground his view was much improved; he could see over the tops of the plants growing by the canal and beyond them to the iridescent towers of Cynia. The towers were not like those of Charax; no two Martian cities looked alike. It was as if each were a unique work of art, each expressing the thoughts of a different artist.

Jim wondered why the towers had been built, what they were good for, how old they were.

The canal crops spread out around them, a dark green sea in which the Martian waded waist deep. The broad leaves were spread flat to the sun's rays, reaching greedily for lifegiving radiant energy. They curled aside as the native's body brushed them, to spread again as he passed.

The towers grew much closer; suddenly the Martian stopped and set the two boys down. He continued to carry Willis. Ahead of them, almost concealed by overhanging greenery, a ramp slanted down into the ground and entered a tunnel arch. Jim looked at it and said, "Frank, what do you think?"

"Gee, I don't know." The boys had been inside the cities of Charax and Copais, but only in the abandoned parts and at ground level. They were not allowed time to fret over their decision; their guide started down the slope at a good clip.

Jim ran after him, shouting, "Hey, Willis!"

The Martian stopped and exchanged a couple of remarks with Willis; the bouncer called out, "Jim wait."

"Tell him to put you down."

"Willis fine. Jim wait." The Martian started up again at a pace that Jim could not possibly match. Jim went disconsolately back to the start of the ramp and sat down on the ledge thereof.

"What are you going to do?" demanded Frank.

"Wait, I suppose. What else can I do? What are *you* going to

"Oh, I'll stick. But I'm not going to miss the scooter."

"Well, neither am I. We couldn't stay here after sundown anyhow."

The precipitous drop in temperature at sunset on Mars is almost all the weather there is, but it means death by freezing for an Earth human unless he is specially clothed and continuously exercising.

They sat and waited and watched spin bugs skitter past. One stopped by Jim's knee, a little tripod of a creature, less than an inch high; it appeared to study him. He touched it; it flung out its limbs and whirled away. The boys were not even alert, since a water-seeker will not come close to a Martian settlement; they simply waited.

Perhaps a half hour later the Martian—or, at least, *a* Martian of the same size—came back. He did not have Willis with him. Jim's face fell. But the Martian said, "Come with me," in his own tongue, prefacing the remark with the question symbol.

"Do we or don't we?" asked Frank.

"We do. Tell him so." Frank complied. The three started down. The Martian laid a great hand flap on the shoulders of each boy and herded him along. Shortly he stopped and picked them up. This time they made no objection.

The tunnel seemed to remain in full daylight even after they had penetrated several hundred yards underground. The light came from everywhere but especially from the ceiling. The tunnel was large by human standards but no more than comfortably roomy for Martians. They passed several other natives; if another was moving their host always boomed a greeting, but if he was frozen in the characteristic trance-like immobility no sound was made.

Once their guide stepped over a ball about three feet in diameter. Jim could not make out what it was at first, then he did a double-take and was still more puzzled. He twisted his neck and looked back at it. It *couldn't be*—but it was!

He was gazing at something few humans ever see, and no human ever wants to see: a Martian folded and rolled into a ball, his hand flaps covering everything but his curved back. Martians—modern, civilized Martians—do not hibernate, but at some time remote eons in the past their ancestors must have done so, for they are still articulated so that they can assume the proper, heat-conserving, moisture-conserving globular shape, if they wish.

They hardly ever so wish.

For a Martian to roll up is the moral equivalent of an Earthly duel to the death and is resorted to only when that Martian is offended so completely that nothing less will suffice. It means: I cast you out, I leave your world, I deny your existence.

The first pioneers on Mars did not understand this, and, through ignorance of Martian values, offended more than once. This delayed human colonization of Mars by many years; it took the most skilled diplomats and semanticians of Earth to repair the unwitting harm. Jim stared unbelievingly at the withdrawn Martian and wondered what could possible have caused him to do that to an entire city. He remembered a grisly tale told him by Doctor MacRae concerning the second expedition to Mars. "So this dumb fool," the doctor had said, "a medical lieutenant he was, though I hate to admit it—this idiot grabs hold of the beggar's flaps and tries to unroll him. Then it happened."

"What happened?" Jim had demanded.

"He disappeared."

"The Martian?"

"No, the medical officer."

"Huh? How did he disappear?"

"Don't ask me; I didn't see it. The witnesses—four of 'em, with sworn statements—say there he was and then there he wasn't. As if he had met a boojum."

"What's a 'boojum'?" Jim had wanted to know.

"You modern kids don't get any education, do you? The boojum is in a book; I'll dig up a copy for you."

"But *how* did he disappear?"

"Don't ask me. Call it mass hypnosis if it makes you feel any better. It makes me feel better, but not much. All I can say is that seven-eighths of an iceberg never shows." Jim had never seen an iceberg, so the allusion was wasted on him—but he felt decidedly *not* better when he saw the rolled up Martian.

"Did you see that?" demanded Frank.

"I wish I hadn't," said Jim. "I wonder what happened?"

"Maybe he ran for mayor and lost."

"It's nothing to joke about. Maybe he—*Sssh!*" Jim broke off.

He caught sight of another Martian, immobile, but not rolled up; politeness called for silence.

The Martian carrying them made a sudden turn to the left and entered a hall; he put them down. The room was very large to them; to Martians it was probably suitable for a cozy social gathering. There were many of the frames they use as a human uses a chair and these were arranged in a circle. The room itself was circular and domed; it had the appearance of being outdoors for the domed ceiling simulated Martian sky, pale blue at the horizon, increasing to to warmer blue, then purple, and reaching purple-black with stars piercing through at the highest point of the ceiling.

A miniature sun, quite convincing, hung west of the meridian. By some trick of perspective the pictured horizons were apparently distant. On the north wall Oeroe seemed to flow past.

Frank's comment was, "Gee whiz!"; Jim did not manage that much.

Their host had placed them by two resting frames. The boys did not attempt to use them; stepladders would have been more comfortable and convenient. The Martian looked first at them, then at the frames, with great sorrowful eyes. He left the room.

He came back very shorly, followed by two others; all three were carrying loads of colorful fabrics. They dumped them down in a pile in the middle of the room. The first Martian picked up Jim and Frank and deposited them gently on the heap.

"I think he means, 'Draw up a chair,' " commented Jim.

The fabrics were not woven but were a continuous sheet, like cobweb, and almost as soft, though much stronger. They were in all hues of all colors from pastel blue to deep, rich red. The boys sprawled on them and waited.

Their host relaxed himself on one of the resting frames; the two others did the same. No one said anything. The two boys were decidedly not tourists; they knew better than to try to hurry a Martian. After a bit Jim got an idea; to test it he cautiously raised his mask. Frank snapped, "Say! What 'cha trying to do? Choke to death?"

Jim left his mask up. "It's all right. The pressure is up."

"It *can't* be. We didn't come through a pressure lock."

"Have it your own way." Jim left his mask up. Seeing that he did not turn blue, gasp, nor become slack-featured, Frank ventured to try it himself. He found himself able to breath without trouble. To be sure, the pressure was not as great as he was used to at home and it would have seemed positively stratospheric to an Earthling, but it was enough for a man at rest.

Several other Martians drifted in and unhurriedly composed themselves on frames. After a while Frank said, "Do you know what's going on, Jim?"

"Uh—maybe."

"No 'maybes' about it. It's a 'growing-together.'"

"Growing together" is an imperfect translation of a Martian idiom which names their most usual social event—in bald terms, just sitting around and saying nothing. In similar terms, violin music has been described as dragging a horse's tail across the dried gut of a cat. "I guess you're right," agreed Jim. "We had better button our lips."

"Sure."

For a long time nothing was said. Jim's thoughts drifted away, to school and what he would do there, to his family, to things in the past. He came back presently to personal self-awareness and realized that he was happier than he had been in a long time, with no particular reason that he could place. It was a quiet happiness; he felt no desire to laugh nor even to smile, but he was perfectly relaxed and content.

He was acutely aware of the presence of the Martians, of each individual Martian, and was becoming even more aware of them with each drifting minute. He had never noticed before how beautiful they were. "Ugly as a native" was a common phrase with the colonials; Jim recalled with surprise that he had even used it himself, and wondered why he ever had done so.

He was aware, too, of Frank beside him and thought about how much he liked him. Staunch—that was the word for Frank, a good man to have at your back. He wondered why he had never told Frank that he liked him.

Mildly he missed Willis, but was not worried about him. This sort of a party was not Willis's dish; Willis liked things noisy, boisterous, and unrefined. Jim put aside the thought of Willis, lay back, and soaked in the joy of living. He noted with delight that the unknown artist who had designed this room had arranged for the miniature sun to move across the ceiling just as the true Sun moved across the sky. He watched it travel to the west and presently begin to drop toward the pictured horizon.

There came a gentle booming behind him—he could not catch the words—and another Martian answered. One of them unfolded himself from his resting stand and ambled out of the room. Frank sat up and said, "I must have been dreaming."

"Did you go to sleep?" asked Jim. "I didn't."

"The heck you didn't. You snored like Doc MacRae."

"Why, I wasn't even asleep."

"Says you!"

The Martian who had left the room returned. Jim was sure it was the same one; they no longer looked alike to him. He was carrying a drinking vase. Frank's eyes bulged out. "Do you suppose they are going to serve us *water?*"

"Looks like," Jim answered in an awed voice.

Frank shook his head. "We might as well keep this to ourselves; nobody'll ever believe us."

"You're right."

The ceremony began. The Martian with the vase announced his own name, barely touched the stem of the vase and passed it on. The next Martian gave his name and also simulated drinking. Around the circle it came. The Martian who had brought them in, Jim learned, was named "Gekko"; it seemed a pretty name to Jim and fitting. At last the vase came around to Jim; a Martian handed it to him with the wish, "May you never suffer thirst." The words were quite clear to him.

There was an answering chorus around him: "May you drink deep whenever you wish!"

Jim took the vase and reflected that Doc said that the Martians didn't have anything that was catching for humans. "Jim Marlowe!" he announced, placed the stem in his mouth and took a sip.

As he handed it back he dug into his imperfect knowledge of the dominant language, concentrated on his accent and managed to say, "May water ever be pure and plentiful for you." There was an approving murmur that warmed him. The Martian handed the vase to Frank.

With the ceremony over the party broke up in noisy, almost human chatter. Jim was trying vainly to follow what was being said to him by a Martian nearly three times his height when Frank said, "Jim! You see that sun? We're going to miss the scooter!"

"Huh? That's not the real Sun; that's a toy."

"No, but it matches the real Sun. My watch says the same thing."

"Oh, for Pete's sake! Where's Willis? Gekko—where's Gekko?"

Gekko, on hearing his name, came over; he clucked inquiringly at Jim. Jim tried very hard to explain their trouble, tripped over syntax, used the wrong directive symbols, lost his accent entirely. Frank shoved him aside and took over. Presently Frank said, "They'll get us there before sunset, but Willis stays here."

"Huh? They can't do that!"

"That's what the man says."

Jim thought. "Tell them to bring Willis here and ask *him*."

Gekko was willing to do that. Willis was carried in, placed upon the floor. He waddled up to Jim and said, "Hi, Jim boy! Hi, Frank boy!"

"Willis," said Jim earnestly, "Jim is going away. Willis come with Jim?"

Willis seemed puzzled. "Stay here. Jim stay here. Willis stay here. Good."

"Willis," Jim said frantically, "Jim has *got* to go away. Willis come with Jim?"

"Jim go?"

"Jim go."

Willis almost seemed to shrug. "Willis go with Jim," he said sadly.

"Tell Gekko." Willis did so. The Martian seemed surprised, but there was no further argument. He gathered up both boys and the bouncer and started for the door. Another larger Martian—tagged "G'kuro" Jim recalled—relieved Gekko of Frank and tailed along behind. As they climbed the tunnel Jim found suddenly that he needed his mask; Frank put his on, too.

The withdrawn Martian was still cluttering the passageway; both their porters stepped over him without comment.

The sun was very low when they got to the surface. Although a Martian cannot be hastened, his normal pace makes very good time; the long-legged pair made nothing of the three miles back to Cynia Station. The sun had just reached the horizon and the air was already bitter when the boys and Willis were dumped on the dock. The two Martians left at once, hurrying back to the warmth of their city.

"Good-by, Gekko!" Jim shouted. "Good-by, G'kuro!"

The driver and the station master were standing on the dock; it was evident that the driver was ready to start and had been missing his passengers. "What in the world?" said the station master.

"We're ready to go," said Jim.

"So I see," said the driver. He stared at the retreating figures. He blinked and turned to the agent. "We should have left that stuff alone, George. I'm seeing things." He added to the boys, "Well, get aboard."

They did so and climbed up to the dome. The car clumped down off the ramp to the surface of the ice, turned left onto Oeroe canal and picked up speed. The Sun dropped behind the horizon; the landscape was briefly illuminated by the short Martian sunset. On each bank the boys could see the plants withdrawing for the night. In a few minutes the ground, so lush with vegetation a half hour before, was bare as the true desert.

The stars were out, sharp and dazzling. Soft curtains of aurora hung over the skyline. In the west a tiny steady light rose and fought its way upwards against the motion of the stars. "There's Phobos," said Frank. "Look!"

"I see it," Jim answered. "It's cold. Let's turn in."

"Okay. I'm hungry."

"I've got some sandwiches left." They munched one each, then went down into the lower compartment and crawled into bunks. In time the car passed the city Hesperidum and turned west-northwest onto the canal Erymanthus, but Jim was unaware of it; Jim was dreaming that Willis and he were singing a duet for the benefit of amazed Martians.

"All out! End of the line!" The driver was prodding them.

"Huh?"

"Up you come, shipmate. This is it—Syrtis Minor."

IV

LOWELL ACADEMY

Dear Mother and Dad,

"The reason I didn't phone you when we got in Wednesday night was that we didn't get in until Thursday morning. When I tried to phone on Thursday the operator told me that Deimos had set for South Colony and then I knew it would be about three days until I could relay a call through Deimos and a letter would get there sooner and save you four and a half credits on a collect phone call. Now I realize that I didn't get this letter off to you right away and maybe you're not going to get it until after I would have been able to make a phone call if I had made it but what you probably don't realize is how busy they keep you at school and how many demands there are on a fellow's time and anyhow you probably heard from Frank's mother that we had gotten here all right and anyway you look at it I still saved you four and one half credits by not making that phone call.

"I can just hear Phyllis saying that I am just hinting that

the half-and-four I saved should be turned over to me but I am not doing anything of the sort because I wouldn't do anything like that and besides I've still got some of the money left that you gave me before I left as well as part of my birthday money and with careful management I will not need any more until you all come through here at Migration even though everything costs more here than it does at home. Frank says it's because they always jack the prices up for the tourist trade but there aren't any tourists around now and won't be until the *Albert Einstein* gets in next week. Anyway if you simply split the difference with me you would still be a clear two and a quarter credits ahead.

"The reason we didn't get here Wednesday night was because the driver decided the ice might not hold so we laid over at Cynia Station and Frank and I just fooled around and killed time until sunset.

"Frank and I have been allowed to room together and we've got a dandy room. It was meant for just one boy and only has one study desk but we're mostly taking the same subjects and lots of times we can use the projector together. I am talking this letter into the study desk recorder because tonight is Frank's night to help out in the kitchen and all I've got left to study is a little bit of history and I'm saving that to do with Frank when he comes back. Professor Steuben says that he does not know what they are going to do if they keep getting more students here with no more room, hang them on hooks maybe but he is just joking. He jokes a lot and everybody likes him and will be sorry when he leaves on the *Albert Einstein* and the new headmaster takes over.

"Well that's all for now because Frank just got back and we had better get to work because tomorrow we have a quiz on system history.

"Your loving son,

"James Madison Marlowe, Jr.

"P.S. Frank just told me that he didn't write his folks either and he wonders if you would mind phoning his mother and telling her that he is all right and would she please send his camera right away, he forgot it.

"P.P.S. Willis sends his love. I just asked him.

P.P.P.S. Tell Phyllis that the girls here are dyeing their hair in stripes. I think it looks silly.

"JIM"

If Professor Otto Steuben, M.A., LL.D., had not retired, Jim's life at Lowell Academy would have been different. But retire he did and went back to San Fernando Valley for a well-earned rest. The entire school went to Marsport to see him off. He shook hands all around and wept a little and commended them to the care of the Marquis Howe, recently arrived from Earth and now taking over.

When Jim and Frank got back from the space port they found the first arrivals gathered around the bulletin board. They crowded in and read the item that was drawing the crowd:

SPECIAL NOTICE

All students are required to keep themselves and their quarters neat and orderly at all times. The supervision of these matters by student monitors has not proved satisfactory. Therefore formal inspections by the Headmaster will be held each week. The first such inspection will be at ten hundred, Saturday, the 7th of Ceres.

(signed) M. Howe, Headmaster

"Well, for crying out loud!" Frank burst out. "What d'you think of that, Jim?"

Jim stared at it darkly. "I think that today is the sixth of Ceres."

"Yeah, but what's the idea? He must think that this is a school of correction." Frank turned to an older student, who had, until, now, been monitor of their corridor. "Anderson, what do you think about it?"

"I really don't know. I thought we were doing all right the way we were."

"What do you intend to do about it?"

"Me?" The young man thought a while before replying,

42

"I've got just one more semester to my degree, then I'm out of here. I think I'll just sit tight, keep my mouth shut, and sweat it out."

"Huh? That's easy enough for you to say but I've got twelve semesters staring me in the face. What am I? A criminal?"

"That's your problem, fellow." The older student left.

One of the boys in the crowd seemed undisturbed by the notice. He was Herbert Beecher, son of the Company's Resident Agent General and a newcomer both to Mars and to the school. One of the other boys noticed his smirk. "What are you looking smug about, tourist?" he demanded. "Did you know about this ahead of time?"

"Certainly I did."

"I'll bet you thought it up."

"No, but my old man says you guys have been getting away with it for a long time. My old man says that Stoobie was too soft to put any discipline into this school. My old man says that——"

"Nobody cares what your old man says. Beat it!"

"You better not talk about my old man that way. I'll——"

"Beat it I said!"

Young Beecher eyed his antagonist—a red-headed lad named Kelly—and decided that he meant it. He faded out of sight.

"He can afford to grin," Kelly said bitterly, "he lives in his old man's quarters. This thing only gets at those of us who have to live in the school. It's rank discrimination, that's what it is!" About a third of boys were day students, mostly sons of Company employees who were stationed at Syrtis Minor. Another third were migratory colonials and the balance were the children of terrestrials at the outlying stations, especially those employed on the atmosphere project. Most of these last were Bolivians and Tibetans, plus a few Eskimos. Kelly turned to one of them. "How about it, Chen? Are we going to put up with this?"

The Asiatic's broad face showed no expression. "It is not worth getting excited about." He started to turn away.

"Huh? You mean you won't stand up for your rights?"

"These things pass."

Jim and Frank went back to their room but continued to discuss it. "Frank," asked Jim, "what's behind this? Do you suppose they're pulling the same stunt over in the girls' school?"

"I could call up Dolores Montez and find out."

"Mmm . . . don't bother. I don't suppose it matters. The question is: what are we going to do about it?"

"What can we do about it?"

"I don't know. I wish I could ask Dad about this. He always told me to stand up for my rights—but maybe he would say that this is just something I should expect. I don't know."

"Look," suggested Frank, "why don't we ask our fathers?"

"You mean call 'em up tonight? Is there relay tonight?"

"No, don't call 'em up; that costs too much. We'll wait till our folks come through here at Migration; that's not so very long now. If we're going to make a fuss, we've got to have our folks here to back us up, or we won't get any place with it. Meantime, we sit tight and do what he asks us. It may not amount to anything."

"Now you're talking sense." Jim stood up. "I suppose we might as well try to get this dump tidied up."

"Okay. Say, Jim, I just thought of something. Isn't the chairman of the Company named Howe?"

"John W. Howe," agreed Jim. "What about it?"

"Well, the head is named Howe, too."

"Oh." Jim shook his head. "Doesn't mean anything. Howe is a very common name."

"I'll bet it does mean something. Doc MacRae says you have to be somebody's cousin to get any of the juicy company appointments. Doc says that the company set-up is just one big happy family, and that the idea that it is a non-profit corporation is the biggest joke since women were invented."

"Hmm . . . Well, I wouldn't know. Where shall I put this junk?"

Slips were distributed at breakfast the next morning giving what was described as "Official Arrangement of Rooms for Inspection"; the job the boys had done the night before had to be done over. Since Headmaster Howe's instructions failed to consider the possibility that two boys might be living in a one-boy room the rearranging was not easy; they were not ready by ten o'clock. However it was nearly two hours later that the Headmaster got around to their cubicle.

He poked his head inside, seemed about to leave, then came inside. He pointed to their outdoors suits, hanging on hooks by the clothes locker. "Why haven't you removed those barbaric decorations from your masks?"

The boys looked startled; Howe went on, "Haven't you looked at the bulletin board this morning?"

"Er—no, sir."

"Do so. You are responsible for anything posted on the bulletin board." He shouted toward the door. "Orderly!"

One of the older students appeared in the doorway. "Yes, sir."

"Weekend privileges suspended for these two pending satisfaction of inspection requirements. Five demerits each." Howe looked around. "This room is unbelievably cluttered and untidy. Why didn't you follow the prescribed diagram?"

Jim stuttered, tongue-tied by the evident unfairness of the question. Finally he got out, "This is supposed to be a single room. We did the best we could."

"Don't resort to excuses. If you don't have room to store things neatly, get rid of the excess baggage." For the first time his eye lit on Willis, who, at the sight of strangers, had retreated to a corner and hauled in all out-rigging. Howe pointed at him. "Athletic equipment must be stored on tops of lockers or left in the gymnasium. It must *not* be thrown in corners."

Jim started to answer; Frank kicked him in a shin. Howe went on lecturing as he moved toward the door. "I realize that you young people have been brought up away from civilization and have not had the benefits of polite society, but I shall do my best to remedy that. I intend that this school shall, above all other things, turn out civilized young gentlemen." He paused at the door and added, "When you have cleaned up those masks, report to my office."

When Howe was out of earshot Jim said, "What did you kick me for?"

"You dumb idiot, he thought Willis was a ball."

"I know; I was just about to set him right."

Frank looked disgusted. "Don't you know enough to let well enough alone? You want to keep Willis, don't you? He would have whipped up some rule making him contraband."

"Oh, he couldn't do that!"

"The heck he couldn't! I'm beginning to see that Stoobie kept our pal Howe from exercising his full talents. Say, what did he mean: 'demerits'?"

"I don't know, but it doesn't sound good." Jim took down his respirator mask, looked at the gay tiger stripes. "You know, Frank, I don't think I want to become a 'civilized young gentleman.'"

"You and me both!"

They decided to take a quick look at the bulletin board before they got into any more trouble, rather than fix the masks at once. They went to the entrance foyer and did so. On the board was pinned:

NOTICE TO STUDENTS

1. The practice of painting respirator masks with so-called identification patterns will cease. Masks will be plain and each student will letter his name neatly in letters one inch high across the chest and across the shoulders of his outdoors suit.

2. Students are required to wear shirts and shoes or slippers at all times and places except in their own rooms.

3. Pets will no longer be permitted. In some cases, where the animals are of interest as scientific specimens, arrangements may be made to feed and care for same in the biology laboratory.

4. Food must not be kept in dormitory rooms. Students receiving food packages from parents will store them with the commissary matron and reasonable amounts may be withdrawn immediately after meals, except Sat-

urday morning breakfast. Special permission may be obtained for "sweet parties" during recreation hours on occasions such as birthdays, etc.

5. Students denied weekend privileges for disciplinary reasons may read, study, compose letters, play musical instruments, or listen to music. They are not permitted to play cards, visit in other students' rooms, nor leave the school area for any reason.

6. Students wishing to place telephone calls will submit a written request on the approved form and will obtain key to the communications booth at the main office.

7. The student council is dissolved. Student government will be resumed only if and when the behavior of the student body justifies it.

(signed) M. Howe, Headmaster

Jim whistled. Frank said, "Would you look at that, Jim? Dissolving the Student Council—imagine that! Do you suppose we have to get permission to scratch? What does he take us for?"

"Search me. Frank, I haven't *got* a shirt."

"Well, I can lend you a sweat shirt until you can buy some. But take a look at paragraph three—you'd better get busy."

"Huh? What about it?" Jim reread it.

"You'd better go butter up the bio teacher, so you can make some arrangements for Willis."

"What?" Jim simply had not connected the injunction concerning pets with Willis; he did not think of Willis as a pet. "Oh, I can't do that, Frank. He'd be terribly unhappy."

"Then you had better ship him home and let your folks care for him."

Jim looked balky. "I won't do it. I won't!"

"Then what are you going to do?"

"I don't know." He thought about it. "I won't do anything about it. I'll just keep him under cover. Howe doesn't even know I've got him."

"Well . . . you might get away with it, so long as nobody snitches on you."

47

"I don't think any of the fellows would do that."

They went back to their room and attempted to remove the decorations from their masks. They were not very successful; the paint had bitten into the plastic and they succeeded only in smearing the colors around. Presently a student named Smythe stuck his head in the door. "Clean up your masks for you?"

"Huh? It can't be done; the colors have soaked in."

"You're the umpteenth to find that out. But, from the goodness of my heart and a willingness to be of public service, I will paint your mask over to match the original shade—at a quarter credit per mask."

"I thought there was a catch in it," Jim answered.

"Do you want it, or don't you? Hurry up, my public is waiting."

"Smitty, you would sell tickets to your grandmother's funeral." Jim produced a quarter credit.

"That's an idea. How much do you think I could charge?" The other boy produced a can of lacquer and a brush, rapidly painted out Jim's proud design, using a pigment that was a fair match for the olive-drab original shade. "There! It'll dry in a couple of minutes. How about you, Sutton?"

"Okay, bloodsucker," Frank agreed.

"Is that any way to talk about your benefactor? I've got a heavy date over on the girls' side and here I am spending my precious Saturday helping you out." Smythe made equally rapid work of Frank's mask.

"Spending your time raising money for your date, you mean," amended Jim. "Smitty, what do you think of these trick rules the new Head has thought up? Should we knuckle under, or make a squawk?"

"Squawk? What for?" Smythe gathered up his tools. "There's a brand-new business opportunity in each one, if you only had the wit to see it. When in doubt, come see Smythe—special services at all hours." He paused at the door. "Don't mention that deal about tickets to my grandmother's funeral; she'd want a cut on it before she kicks off. Granny is a very shrewd gal with a credit."

"Frank," remarked Jim when Smythe was gone, "there is something about that guy I don't like."

Frank shrugged. "He fixed us up. Let's check in and get off the punishment list."

"Right. He reminds me of something Doc used to say. 'Every law that was ever written opened up a new way to graft.' "

"That's not necessarily so. Come on."

They found a long line waiting outside the Headmaster's office. They were finally ushered in in groups of ten. Howe gave their masks a brief glance each, then started in to lecture. "I hope that this will be a lesson to you young gentle-en not only in neatness, but in alertness. Had you noticed what was posted on the bulletin board you would have been, each of you, prepared for inspection. As for the dereliction itself, I want you to understand that this lesson far transcends the matter of the childish and savage designs you have been using on your face coverings, offensive as they were."

He paused and made sure of their attention. "There is actually no reason why colonial manners should be rude and vulgar and, as head of this institution, I intend to see to it that whatever defects there may have been in your home backgrounds are repaired. The first purpose, perhaps the only purpose, of education is the building of character—and character can be built only through discipline. I flatter myself that I am exceptionally well prepared to undertake this task; before coming here I had twelve years' experience as a master at the Rocky Mountains Military Academy, an exceptionally fine school, a school that produced *men.*"

He paused again, either to catch his breath or let his words soak in. Jim had come in prepared to let a reprimand roll off his back, but the schoolmaster's supercilious attitude and most especially his suggestion that a colonial home was an inferior sort of environment had gradually gotten his dander up. He spoke up. "Mr. Howe?"

"Eh? Yes? What is it?"

"This is not the Rocky Mountains; it's Mars. And this isn't a military academy."

There was a brief moment when it seemed as if Mr.

Howe's surprise and anger might lead him to some violence, or even to apoplexy. After a bit he contained himself and said through tight lips, "What is your name?"

"Marlowe, sir. James Marlowe."

"It would be a far, far better thing for you, Marlowe, if it were a military academy." He turned to the others. "The rest of you may go. Weekend privileges are restored. Marlowe, remain behind."

When the others had left Howe said, "Marlowe, there is nothing in this world more offensive than a smart-aleck boy, an ungrateful upstart who doesn't know his place. You are enjoying a fine education through the graciousness of the Company. It ill behooves you to make cheap wisecracks at persons appointed by the Company to supervise your training and welfare. Do you realize that?"

Jim said nothing. Howe said sharply, "Come! Speak up, lad—admit your fault and make your apology. Be a man!"

Jim still said nothing. Howe drummed on the desk top; finally he said, "Very well, go to your room and think it over. You have the weekend to think about it."

When Jim got back to his room Frank looked him over and shook his head admiringly. "Boy, oh boy!" he said, "ain't you the reckless one."

"Well, he needed to be told."

"He sure did. But what are your plans now? Are you going to cut your throat, or just enter a monastery? Old Howie will be gunning for you every minute from here on out. Matter of fact, it won't be any too safe to be your roommate."

"Confound it, Frank, if that's the way you feel, you're welcome to find another roommate!"

"Easy, easy! I won't run out on you. I'm with you to the end. 'Smiling, the boy fell dead.' I'm glad you told him off. I wouldn't have had the courage to do it myself."

Jim threw himself across his bunk. "I don't think I can stand this place. I'm not used to being pushed around and sneered at, just for nothing. And now I'm going to get it double. What can I do?"

"Derned if I know."

"This was a nice place under old Stoobie. I thought I was going to like it just fine."

"Stoobie was all right. But what *can* you do, Jim, except shut up, take it, and hope he will forget it?"

"Look, nobody else likes it either. Maybe if we stood together we could make him slow up."

"Not likely. You were the only one who had the guts to speak up. Shucks, *I* didn't even back you up—and I agree with you a hundred per cent."

"Well, suppose we all sent letters to our parents?"

Frank shook his head. "You couldn't get them all to—and some pipsqueak would snitch. Then you would be in the soup, for inciting to riot or some such nonsense. Anyhow," he went on, "just what could you say in a letter that you could put your finger on and prove that Mr. Howe was doing something he had no right to? I know what my old man would say."

"What would he say?"

"Many's the time he's told me stories about the school he went to back Earthside and what a rough place it was. I think he's a little bit proud of it. If I tell him that Howie won't let us keep cookies in our room, he'll just laugh at me. He'd say——"

"Dawggone it, Frank, it's not the rule about food in our rooms; it's the whole picture."

"Sure, sure. *I* know it. But try to tell my old man. All we can tell is little things like that. It'll have to get a lot worse before you could get our parents to do anything."

Frank's views were confirmed as the day wore on. As the news spread student after student dropped in on them, some to pump Jim's hand for having bearded the Headmaster, some merely curious to see the odd character who had had the temerity to buck vested authority. But one two-pronged fact became apparent: no one liked the new school head and all resented some or all of his new "disciplinary" measures, but no one was anxious to join up in what was assumed to be a foregone lost cause.

On Sunday Frank went out into Syrtis Minor—the terrestrial settlement, not the nearby Martian city. Jim, under what amounted to room arrest, stayed in their room, pretended to study and talked to Willis. Frank came back at supper time and announced, "I brought you a present." He chucked Jim a tiny package.

"You're a pal! What is it?"

"Open it and see."

It was a new tango recording, made in Rio and direct from Earth via the *Albert Einstein,* titled *¿Quién Es La Señorita?* Jim was inordinately fond of Latin music; Frank had remembered it.

"Oh, boy!" Jim went to the study desk, threaded the tape into the speaker, and got ready to enjoy it. Frank stopped him.

"There's the supper bell. Better wait."

Reluctantly Jim complied, but he came back and played it several times during the evening until Frank insisted that they study. He played it once more just before lights-out.

The dormitory corridor had been dark and quiet for perhaps fifteen minutes when *¿Quién Es La Señorita?* started up again. Frank sat up with a start. "What the dickens? Jim —don't play that now!"

"I'm not," protested Jim. "It must be Willis. It has to be Willis."

"Well, shut him up. Choke him. Put a pillow over his head."

Jim switched on the light. "Willis boy—hey, Willis! Shut up that racket!" Willis probably did not even hear him. He was standing in the middle of the floor, beating time with his eye stalks, and barrelling on down the groove. His rendition was excellent, complete with marimbas and vocal chorus.

Jim picked him up. "Willis! Shut up, fellow."

Willis kept on beating it out.

The door burst open and framed Headmaster Howe. "Just as I thought," he said triumphantly, "no consideration for other people's rights and comforts. Shut off that speaker. And consider yourself restricted to your room for the next month."

Willis kept on playing; Jim tried to hide him with his

body. "Didn't you hear my order?" demanded Howe. "I said to shut off that music." He strode over to the study desk and twisted the speaker switch. Since it was already shut off full, all he accomplished was breaking a fingernail. He suppressed an unschoolmasterly expression and stuck the finger in his mouth. Willis worked into the third chorus.

Howe turned around. "How do you have this thing wired?" he snapped. Getting no answer, he stepped up to Jim and said, "What are you hiding?" He shoved Jim aside, looked at Willis with evident disbelief and distaste. "What is *that?*"

"Uh, that's Willis," Jim answered miserably, raising his voice to be heard.

Howe was not entirely stupid; it gradually penetrated that the music he had been hearing came out of the curious-looking, fuzzy sphere in front of him.

"And what is 'Willis,' may I ask?"

"Well, he's a . . . a bouncer. A sort of a Martian." Willis picked this moment to finish the selection, breathe a liquid contralto *buenas noches*, and shut up—for the moment.

"A bouncer? I've never heard of one."

"Well, not very many have seen one, even among the colonists. They're scarce."

"Not scarce enough. Sort of a Martian parrot, I assume."

"Oh, no!"

"What do you mean, 'Oh, no'?"

"He's not a bit like a parrot. He talks, he thinks—he's my friend!"

Howe was over his surprise and recalling the purpose of his visit. "All that is beside the point. You saw my order about pets?"

"Yes, but Willis is not a pet."

"What is he, then?"

"Well, he *can't* be a pet. Pets are animals; they're property. Willis isn't property; he's—well, he's just Willis."

Willis picked this time to continue with the next thing he had heard after the last playing of the tango. "Boy, when I hear that music," he remarked in Jim's voice, "I don't even remember that old no-good Howe."

"I can't forget him," Willis went on in Frank's voice. "I

wish I had had the nerve to tell him off the same time you did, Jim. You know what? I think Howe is nuts, I mean really nuts. I'll bet he was a coward when he was a kid and it's twisted him inside."

Howe turned white. Frank's arm-chair psychoanalyzing had hit dead center. He raised his hand as if to strike, then dropped it again, uncertain what to strike. Willis hastily withdrew all protuberances and became a smooth ball.

"I say it's a pet," he said savagely, when he regained his voice. He scooped Willis up and headed for the door.

Jim started after him. "Say! Mr. Howe—you can't take Willis!"

The Headmaster turned. "Oh, I can't, can't I? You get back to bed. See me in my office in the morning."

"If you hurt Willis, I'll . . . I'll——"

"You'll what?" He paused. "Your precious pet won't be hurt. Now you get back in that bed before I thrash you." He turned again and left without stopping to see whether or not his order had been carried out.

Jim stood staring at the closed door, tears streaming down his cheeks, sobs of rage and frustration shaking him. Frank came over and put a hand on him. "Jim. Jim, don't take on so. You heard him promise not to hurt Willis. Get back into bed and settle it in the morning. At the very worst you'll have to send Willis home."

Jim shook off the hand.

Frank went on, "Don't let him get your goat, fellow; if he gets you angry, you'll do something silly and then he's got you."

"I'm already angry."

"I know you are and I don't blame you. But you've got to get over it and use your head. He was laying for you— you saw that. No matter what he does or says you've got to keep cool and outsmart him—or he gets you in wrong."

"I suppose you're right."

"I know I'm right. That's what Doc would say. Now come to bed."

Neither one of them got much sleep that night. Toward morning Jim had a nightmare that Howe was a withdrawn

Martian whom he was trying to unroll—against his better judgment.

There was a brand-new notice on the bulletin board at breakfast time. It read:

IMPORTANT NOTICE

Hereafter all personal weapons will be kept in the armory at all times. The office of student armorer is abolished; weapons will be issued by the Headmaster and only when the student concerned is leaving the limits of the school and the adjoining settlement. The practice of wearing sidearms in areas where there is no actual danger from Martian *fauna* will cease.

(signed) M. Howe, Headmaster

Jim and Frank read it together. "I don't get it," said Jim. "Why should he want to take over such a headache? Especially since most of us are licensed?" All the students usually kept their guns in the armory, but the student armorer had kept check only on the weapons of those students still trying to win their licenses.

Frank studied it. "Do you know what I think?"

"No. What?"

"I think he's afraid of you personally."

"Me? Why?"

"Because of what happened last night. There was murder in your eye and he saw it. I think he wants to pull your teeth. I don't think he gives a hoot about the rest of us hanging on to our guns."

"You really think so? Hmm . . . maybe it's a good thing our guns don't happen to be in the armory at the moment."

"The question is: what are you going to do about it?"

Jim thought about it. "I'm not going to give up my gun. Dad wouldn't want me to. I'm sure of that. Anyhow, I'm licensed and I don't have to. I'm a qualified marksman, I've passed the psycho tests, and I've taken the oath; I'm as much entitled to wear a gun as he is."

"Okay, I'm with you on it. But we had better think up a wrinkle before you have to go see him this morning."

The wrinkle showed up at breakfast—the student named Smythe. Frank spoke to Jim about it in a low voice; together they accosted the student after breakfast and brought him to their room. "Look, Smitty," began Jim, "you're a man with lots of angles, aren't you?"

"Mmm . . . could be. What's up?"

"You saw that notice this morning?"

"Sure. Who didn't? Everybody is grousing about it."

"Are you going to turn in your gun?"

"My gun has been in the armory all along. What do I need a gun for around here? I've got a brain."

"In that case you won't be called in about your gun. Now just supposing that you were handed two packages to take care of. You won't open them and you won't know what's in them. Do you think you could find a safe, a *really* safe place to keep them and still be able to give them back on short notice?"

"I don't suppose you want me to tell anybody about these, uh, packages?"

"Nope. Nobody."

"Hmm . . . this sort of service comes high."

"How high?"

"Well, now, I couldn't afford to do it for less than two credits a week."

"That's too much," Frank put in sharply.

"Well—you're friends of mine. I'll make you a flat rate of eight credits for the rest of the year."

"Too much."

"Six credits then, and I won't go lower. You've got to pay for the risk."

"It's a deal," Jim said before Frank could bargain further.

Smythe left with a bundle before Jim reported to the Headmaster's office.

V

LITTLE PITCHERS HAVE BIG EARS

HEADMASTER HOWE kept Jim waiting thirty minutes before admitting him. When he was finally let in, Jim saw that Howe seemed to be quite pleased with himself. He glanced up. "Yes? You asked to see me?"

"You told me to see you, sir."

"I did? Let me see now, what is your name?"

He darn well knows my name, Jim said savagely to himself; *he's trying to get my goat.* He recalled Frank's solemn warning not to lose his temper. "James Marlowe, sir," he answered evenly.

"Oh, yes. Now, Marlowe, you wanted to see me about something?"

"You told me to see you. About Willis."

"Willis? Oh, yes, the Martian roundhead." Howe smiled with his lips. "An interesting scientific specimen."

Howe added nothing more. The silence kept up so long that Jim began to realize that the Headmaster intended to force him to make any moves. Jim had already resigned himself to the idea that it would be impossible to keep Willis at the school any longer. He said, "I've come to get him. I'm going to take him out in town and arrange to send him home."

Howe smiled more broadly. "Oh, you are? And pray tell me how you are going to do that when you are restricted to the school for the next thirty days?"

Frank was still warning him; Jim could almost hear him. He answered, "All right, sir, I'll get somebody to do it for me—today. Now, please, can I have Willis?"

Howe leaned back and crossed his fingers over his stomach. "You bring up a most interesting point, Marlowe. You said last night that this creature is not a pet."

Jim was puzzled. "Yes?"

"You were quite emphatic about it. You said that he wasn't your property, but your friend. That's right, isn't it?"

Jim hesitated. He could feel that a trap was being built for him, but he was not sure what sort. "What if I did?"

"Did you say that, or didn't you? Answer me!"

"Well—yes."

Howe leaned forward. "In that case, what are you doing in here demanding that I turn this creature over to you? You have no claim on him."

"But—but—" Jim stopped, at a loss for words. He had been tricked with words, slippery words; he did not know how to answer them. "You can't do that!" he blurted out. "You don't own him, either! You have no right to keep him locked up."

Howe carefully fitted his finger tips together. "That is a matter still to be determined. Although you have waived all claim to him, it may be that the creature is property nevertheless—in which case he was found on the school grounds and I may take title to him on behalf of the school, as a scientific specimen."

"But—You can't do that; that's not fair! If he belongs to anybody, he belongs to me! You've got no right to——"

"Silence!" Jim shut up; Howe went on more quietly, "Don't tell me what I can or cannot do. You forget that I am *in loco parentis* to you. Any rights that you may have are vested in me, just as if I were your own father. As to the disposition of this creature, I am looking into it; I expect to see the Agent General this afternoon. In due course you will be informed of the outcome."

The Latin phrase confused Jim, as it was intended to; but he did catch one point in Howe's statement and snatched at it. "I'm going to tell my father about this. You can't get away with it."

"Threats, eh?" Howe smiled sourly. "Don't bother to ask for the key to the communications booth; I don't propose to have students phoning their parents every time I tell them to wipe their noses. Send your father a letter—but let me hear it before you send it." He stood up. "That is all. You may go."

Frank was waiting. "I don't see any blood," he announced, looking Jim over. "How did it go?"

"Oh, that so-and-so!"

"Bad, eh?"

"Frank, he won't let me have Willis."

"He's going to make you send him home? But you expected that."

"No, not that. He won't let me have him at all. He used a lot of double-talk but all it meant was that he had him and meant to keep him." Jim seemed about to break down and blubber. "Poor little Willis—you know how timid he is. Frank, what'll I do?"

"I don't get it," Frank answered slowly. "He can't keep Willis, not for keeps. Willis belongs to you."

"I told you he used a lot of double-talk—but that's what he means to do just the same. How am I going to get him back? Frank, I've just got to get him back."

Frank did not answer; Jim looked around disconsolately and noticed the room for the first time. "What happened here?" he asked. "The place looks like you had tried to wreck it."

"Oh, that. I started to tell you. While you were gone, a couple of Howie's stooges searched the place."

"Huh?"

"Trying to find our guns. I just played dumb."

"They did, did they?" Jim appeared to make up his mind. "I've got to find Smythe." He headed for the door.

"Hey, wait—what d'you want to find Smitty for?"

Jim looked back and his face was very old. "I'm going to get my gun and go back there and get Willis."

"Jim! You're nuts!"

Jim did not answer but continued toward the door.

Frank stuck out a foot, tripped him and landed on his back as he went down. He grabbed Jim's right arm and twisted it behind his back. "Now you just rest there," he told Jim, "until you quiet down."

"Let me up."

"You got some sense in your head?"

No answer. "Okay," Frank went on, "I can sit here just as long as you want to. Let me know when you've quieted down." Jim started to struggle; Frank twisted his arm until he yelped and relaxed.

"That's better," said Frank. "Now listen to me: you're a nice guy, Jim, but you go off half-cocked. Suppose you do get your gun and suppose you manage to scare old Howie into coughing up Willis. How long are you going to keep him? You know how long? Just long enough for him to call in some Company police. Then they lock you up and take Willis away from you again. And you'll never see Willis again, not to mention the trouble and grief you'll cause your folks."

There followed a considerable silence. Finally Jim said, "Okay, let me up."

"You've given up the idea of waving your gun around?"

"Sure."

"On your honor? Licensed gun-wearer's oath and all that sort of thing?"

"Yes, I promise."

Frank let him up and brushed him off. Jim rubbed his arm and said, "You needn't have twisted it so hard."

"You're a fine one to complain; you ought to thank me. Now grab your notebook; we're going to be late to chemistry lab."

"I'm not going."

"Don't be silly, Jim. No use to pile up a bunch of cuts and maybe flunk just because you're sore at the Head."

"That's the the idea. I'm quitting, Frank. I won't stay in this school."

"What? Don't be hasty, Jim. I know how you feel, but it's here or nowhere. Your folks can't afford to send you back to Earth for school."

"Then it's nowhere. I won't stay here. I'm going to hang around just long enough to find some way to get my hands on Willis, then I'm going home."

"Well . . ." Frank stopped to scratch his head. "It's your

problem. But see here—you might as well come on to chem lab. It won't hurt you any and you don't intend to leave this minute anyhow."

"No."

Frank looked worried. "Will you promise me to stay right here and not do anything rash till I get back?"

"Why should you worry?"

"Promise me, Jim, or I cut lab, too."

"Oh, all right, all right! Go ahead."

"Right!" Frank dashed away.

When Frank got back he found Jim sprawled on his bunk. "Asleep?"

"No."

"Figured out what you are going to do?"

"No."

"Anything you want?"

"No."

"Your conversation is brilliant," Frank commented and sat down at the study desk.

"Sorry." Nothing was heard from Howe the rest of that day. Frank managed to persuade Jim to attend classes the next day by pointing out that he did not want to invite attention to himself while he was waiting for an opportunity to grab Willis.

Tuesday also passed without word from Howe. Tuesday night, perhaps two hours after lights-out, Frank suddenly woke up. Someone was stirring in the room. "Jim!" he called out softly.

Dead silence. Keeping quiet himself Frank reached out and switched on the light. Jim was standing near the door. "Jim," complained Frank, "why didn't you answer me? You trying to scare me to death?"

"Sorry."

"What's up? What are you doing out of bed?"

"Never mind. You go on back to sleep."

Frank climbed out of bed. "Oh, no! Not while you've got that wild look in your eye. Now tell papa."

Jim waved him away. "I don't want to mix you up in this. Go on back to bed."

"Think you're big enough to make me? Now cut out the foolishness and give. What are your plans?"

Reluctantly Jim explained. It seemed likely to him that Headmaster Howe had Willis locked up somewhere in his office. Jim planned to break in and attempt a rescue. "Now you go back to bed," he finished. "If they question you, you don't know anything; you slept all night."

"Let you tackle it alone? Not likely! Anyhow you need somebody to jigger for you." Frank started fumbling around in their locker.

"I don't want any help. What are you looking for?"

"Laboratory gloves," answered Frank. "You're going to get help whether you want it or not, you thumb-fingered idiot. I don't want you caught."

"What do you want gloves for?"

"Ever hear of finger prints?"

"Sure, but he'll know who did it—and I don't care; I'll be gone."

"Sure, he'll know, but he may not be able to prove it. Here, put these on." Jim accepted the gloves and with them he tacitly accepted Frank's help in the adventure.

Burglarly is not common on Mars and locks are unusual items. As for night watchmen, manpower is not transported through millions of miles of space simply to be used to watch the silent corridors of a boys' school. The principal hazard that Jim and Frank faced in getting to the school's offices was the chance of running into some restless student going to the washroom after hours.

They moved as silently as possibly and scouted each stretch of corridor before entering it. In a few minutes they were at the outer door of the offices without—they hoped—having been seen. Jim tried the door; it was locked. "Why do they bother to lock this?" he whispered.

"On account of guys like you and me," Frank told him. "Go back to the corner and keep your eye peeled." He attacked the latch with his knife.

"Okay." Jim went to the passageway intersection and kept lookout. Five minutes later Frank hissed at him; he went back. "What's the matter?"

"Nothing's the matter. Come on." Frank had the outer door open.

They tiptoed through the outer office, past recording desks and high stacked spool files to an inner door marked: Marquis Howe—HEADMASTER—*Private*.

The lettering on the door was new—and so was the lock. The lock was no mere gesture, capable of being picked or sprung with a knife; it was a combination type, of titanium steel, and would have looked more at home on a safe.

"Think you can open it?" Jim asked anxiously.

Frank whistled softly. "Don't be silly. The party is over, Jim. Let's see if we can get back to bed without getting caught."

"Maybe we can get the door off its hinges."

"It swings the wrong way. I'd rather try to cut a hole through the partition." He moved aside, knelt down, and tried the point of his knife on the wall.

Jim looked things over. There was an air-conditioning duct running from the corridor through the room they were in and to the wall of the headmaster's office. The hole for the duct was almost as wide as his shoulders; if he could unscrew the holding flanges and let the duct sag out of the way——

No, he could not even get up to it; there was nothing to use as a ladder. The file cabinets were fastened to the floor, he found.

There was a small grille set in the bottom of the door, to permit the exhaust air to escape from the inner office. It could not be removed, nor would the hole left be large enough to be of use, but he lay down and tried to peer through it. He could see nothing; the room beyond was dark.

He cupped his hands over it and called out, "Willis! Oh, Willis! Willis boy——"

Frank came over and said urgently, "Cut that out. Are you trying to get us caught?"

"Sh!" Jim put his ear to the grille.

They both heard a muffled reply: "Jim boy! Jim!"

Jim replied, "Willis! Come here, Willis!" and listened. "He's in there," he said to Frank. "Shut up in something."

"Obviously," agreed Frank. "Now will you quiet down before somebody comes?"

"We've got to get him out. How are you making out with the wall?"

"No good. There's heavy wire mesh set in the plastic."

"Well, we've got to get him out. What do we do?"

"We don't do a darn thing," asserted Frank. "We're stymied. We go back to bed."

"You can go back to bed if you want to. I'm going to stay here and get him out."

"The trouble with you, Jim, is that you don't know when you are licked. Come on!"

"No. Sh!" He added, "Hear anything?"

Frank listened. "I hear something. What is it?"

It was a scraping noise from inside the inner office. "It's Willis, trying to get out," Jim stated.

"Well, he can't. Let's go."

"No." Jim continued to listen at the grille. Frank waited impatiently, his spirit of adventure by now more than satisfied. He was stretched between a reluctance to run out on Jim and an anxiety to get back to his room before they were caught. The scraping noise continued.

After a while it stopped. There was a soft *plop!* as if something soft but moderately heavy had fallen a foot or so, then there was a slight scurrying sound, almost beyond hearing.

"Jim? Jim boy?"

"Willis!" yelped Jim. The bouncer's voice had come to him from just beyond the grille.

"Jim boy take Willis home."

"Yes, yes! Stay there, Willis; Jim has to find a way to get Willis out."

"Willis get out." The bouncer stated it positively.

"Frank," Jim said urgently, "if we could just find something to use as a crowbar, I could bust that grille out of its frame. I think maybe Willis could squeeze through."

"We've got nothing like that. We've got nothing but our knives."

"Think, fellow, think! Is there anything in our room, anything at all?"

"Not that I know of." The scraping noise had resumed; Frank added, "What's Willis up to?"

"I guess he's trying to get the door open. We've got to find some way to open it for him. Look, I'll boost you up on my shoulders and you try to take the collar off that air duct."

Frank looked the situation over. "No good. Even if we get the duct down, there'll be a grille set in the other side of the wall."

"How do you know?"

"There always is."

Jim shut up. Frank was certainly correct and he knew it. The scraping sound had continued, still continued. Frank dropped on one knee and put his head close to the grille. He listened.

"Take it easy," he advised Jim after a moment. "I think maybe Willis is making out all right by himself."

"What do you mean?"

"That's a cutting sound if I ever heard one."

"Huh? Willis can't cut through a door. Many's the time I've locked him up, back home."

"Maybe. Maybe not. Maybe he just didn't want to get out bad enough." The scraping sound was more distinct now.

A few minutes later a fine circular line began to show around the grille, then the portion of the door enclosed by the line fell toward them. For an instant Willis could be seen through the hole. Sticking out from his tubby body was a clawed pseudolimb eight inches long and an inch thick. "What's that?" demanded Frank.

"Darned if I know. He never did anything like *that* before."

The strange limb withdrew, disappeared inside his body, and the fur closed over the spot, leaving no sign that it had ever existed. Willis proceeded to change his shape, until he was more nearly watermelon-shaped than globular. He oozed through the hole. "Willis out," he announced proudly.

Jim snatched him up and cradled him in his arms. "Willis! Willis, old fellow."

The bouncer cuddled in his arms. "Jim boy lost," he said accusingly. "Jim went away."

"Yes, but not ever again. Willis stay with Jim."

"Willis stay. Good."

Jim rubbed his cheek against the little fellow's fur. Frank cleared his throat. "It might be a good idea to pop back into our hole."

"Sure." The trip back to their room was made quickly and, so far as they could detect, without arousing attention. Jim dumped Willis on his bed and looked around. "I wonder just what I should try to take? I'll have to get hold of Smitty and get my gun."

"Hold on," said Frank. "Don't get ahead of yourself. You don't really have to go, you know."

"Huh?"

"I didn't hurt the outer lock; we never touched Howe's private lock. All there is to show for Willis's escape is a hole that we obviously couldn't get through—and another one like it, probably, in Howe's desk. He can't prove a thing. You can arrange to ship Willis back and we can just sit tight."

Jim shook his head. "I'm leaving. Willis is just part of it. I wouldn't stay in a school run by Howe if you paid me to."

"Why be hasty, Jim?"

"I'm not being hasty. I don't blame you for staying; in another year you can take the rocket pilot candidate exams and get out. But if you should happen to bust the exams, I'll bet you don't stick here until graduation."

"No, I probably won't. Have you figured out how you are going to get away without Howe stopping you? You don't dare leave until daylight; it is too cold until then."

"I'll wait until daylight and just walk out."

"The idea," Frank said dryly, "is to get away. What you want to do is to pull a sneak. I think we had better find a way to keep you under cover until that can be arranged. The chances ought to be good after noon."

Jim was about to ask Frank why he thought the chances would be good after noon when Willis repeated the last three words. First he repeated them in Frank's voice, then he said them again in rich, fruity accents of an older man. "Good afternoon!" he intoned.

"Shut up, Willis."

Willis said it again, "Good afternoon, Mark. Sit down, my boy. Always happy to see you."

"I've heard that voice," said Frank, puzzlement in his tones.

"Thank you, General. How do you do, sir?" Willis went on, now in the precise, rather precious tones of Headmaster Howe.

"I know!" said Frank. "I've heard it on broadcast; it's Beecher, the Resident Agent General."

"Sh—" said Jim, "I want to listen." Willis continued, again in the fruity voice:

"Not bad, not too bad for an old man."

"Nonsense, General, you're not old."—Howe's voice again.

"Kind of you to say so, my boy," Willis went on. "What have you in the bag? Contraband?"

Willis repeated Howe's sycophantic laugh. "Hardly. Just a scientific specimen—a rather interesting curiosity I confiscated from one of the students."

There was a short pause, then the fruity voice said, "Bless my boots! Mark, wherever did you find this creature?"

"I just told you, sir," came Howe's voice. "I was forced to take it away from one of the students."

"Yes, yes—but do you have any idea of *what* you've got?"

"Certainly, sir; I looked it up. *Areocephalopsittacus Bron*——"

"Spare me the learned words, Mark. It's a roundhead, a Martian roundhead. That's not the point. You say you got this from a student; do you think you could buy it from him?" the fruity voice continued eagerly.

Howe's voice answered slowly, "I hardly think so, sir. I am fairly sure he wouldn't want to sell." He hesitated, then went on, "Is it important?"

"Important? That depends on what you mean by 'important,' " answered the voice of the Resident Agent General. "Would you say that sixty thousand credits was important? Or even seventy thousand? For that is what I am sure the London zoo will pay for him, over and above the cost of getting him there."

"Really?"

"Really. I have a standing order from a broker in London at fifty thousand credits; I've never been able to get him one. I'm sure the price can be boosted."

"Indeed?" Howe agreed cautiously. "That would be a fine thing for the Company, wouldn't it?"

There was a brief silence, then a hearty laugh. "Mark, my boy, you slay me. Now see here—you are hired to run the school, aren't you?"

"Yes."

"And I'm hired to look out for the interests of the Company, right? We put in a good day's work and earn our pay; that leaves eighteen hours a day that belongs to each of us, personally. Are you hired to find strange specimens?"

"No."

"Neither am I. Do you understand me?"

"I think I do."

"I'm sure you do. After all, I know your uncle quite well; I'm sure he wouldn't have sent his nephew out here without explaining the facts of life to him. He understands them very well himself, I can assure you. The fact is, my boy, that there are unlimited opportunities in a place such as this for a smart man, if he will just keep his eyes and ears open. Not graft, you understand." Willis paused.

Jim started to say something; Frank said, "Shut up! We don't want to miss any of this."

The Resident's voice continued, "Not graft at all. Legitimate business opportunities that are the natural concomitants of our office. Now about this student: what will it take to convince him he should sell? I wouldn't offer him too much or he will become suspicious. We mustn't have that."

Howe was slow in replying. "I am almost certain he won't sell, General, but there is another way, possibly."

"Yes? I don't understand you."

The boys heard Howe explain his peculiar theory of ownership with respect to Willis. They could not see Beecher dig Howe in the ribs but they could hear his choked laughter. "Oh, that is rich! Mark, you slay me, you really do. Your talents are wasted as a school teacher; you should be a resident."

"Well," Howe's voice replied, "I hardly expect to teach school all my life."

"You won't, you won't. We'll find an agency for you. After all, the school will be smaller and of less importance after the non-migration policy goes into effect."

("What's he talking about?" whispered Frank—"Quiet!" Jim answered.)

"Is there any news about that?" Howe wanted to know.

"I expect to hear from your uncle momentarily. You might stop in again this evening, my boy; I may have news."

The remainder of the conversation was of no special interest, but Willis plowed on with it nevertheless. The boys listened until Howe had made his farewell, after which Willis shut up.

Jim was frothing. "Put Willis in a zoo! Why, the very idea! I hope he does catch me leaving; I'd welcome an excuse to take a shot at him!"

"Easy, fellow! I wonder," Frank went on, "what that business was about a 'non-migration' policy?"

"I thought he said 'immigration'. What time is it?"

"About three."

"We've got three hours, more or less. Jim, let's see what else we can coax out of Willis. I've got a hunch it may be important."

"Okay." Jim picked the fuzz ball up and said, "Willis old fellow, what else do you know? Tell Jim everything you've heard—*every*thing."

Willis was happy to oblige. He reeled off bits of dialogue for the next hour, most of it concerned with unimportant routine of the school. At last the boys were rewarded by hearing again the unctuous tones of Gaines Beecher:

"Mark, my boy——"

"Oh—come in, General. Sit down. Happy to see you."

"I just stopped by to say that I have gotten a dispatch from your dear uncle. He added a postscript sending his regards to you."

"That's nice. Thank you, sir."

"Not at all. Close that door, will you?" Willis put in sound effects of a door being closed. "Now we can talk. The dispatch, of course, concerned the non-migration policy."

"Yes?"

"I am happy to say that the board came around to your uncle's point of view. South Colony will stay where it is; this next ship load and the one following it will go to North Colony, where the new immigrants will have nearly twelve months of summer in which to prepare for the northern winter. What are you chuckling about?"

"Nothing important, sir. One of the students, a great lout named Kelly, was telling me today what his father was going to do to me when he came through here at migration. I am looking forward to seeing his face when he learns that his father will not show up."

"You are not to tell him anything of the sort," the Resident's voice said sharply.

"Eh?"

"I want all this handled with the least possible friction. No one must know until the last possible moment. There are hotheads among the colonials who will oppose this policy, even though it has already been proved that, with reasonable precautions, the dangers of a Martian winter are negligible. My plan is to postpone migration two weeks on some excuse, then postpone it again. By the time I announce the change it will be too late to do anything but comply."

"Ingenious!"

"Thank you. It's really the only way to handle colonials, my boy. You haven't been here long enough to know them the way I do. They are a neurotic lot, most of them failures back on Earth, and they will drive you wild with their demands if you are not firm with them. They don't seem to understand that all that they are and all that they have they owe directly to the Company. Take this new policy: if you let the colonists have their own way, they would continue to follow the sun, like so many rich playboys—and at the Company's expense."

Willis shifted to Howe's voice. "I quite agree. If their children are any guide, they are a rebellious and unruly lot."

"Really shiftless," agreed the other voice. "You must be firm with them. I must be going. Oh, about that, uh, specimen: you have it in a safe place?"

"Yes indeed, sir. Locked in this cabinet."

"Hmm . . . it might be better to bring it to my quarters."

"Hardly necessary," Howe's voice denied. "Notice the lock on that door? It will be safe."

There were good-byes said and Willis shut up.

Frank muttered savagely to himself.

VI

FLIGHT

JIM SHOOK HIM by the shoulder. "Snap out of it and help me. I'm going to be late."

Frank said softly, "I wonder how he would like to tackle a winter at Charax? Maybe *he'd* like to stay inside for eleven or twelve months at a time—or go outside when it's a hundred below."

"Sure, sure," agreed Jim. "But give me a hand."

Frank turned suddenly and took down Jim's outdoors suit. He flung it at him, then took down his own and started climbing rapidly into it. Jim stared. "Hey—what you doing?"

"I'm going with you."

"Huh?"

"Think I'm going to sit here and do lessons when somebody is planning to trick my mother into being forced to last out a high-latitude winter? My own mother? Mom's got a bad heart; it would kill her." He turned and started digging things out of the locker. "Let's get moving."

Jim hesitated, then said, "Sure, Frank, but how about your plans? If you quit school now you'll never be a rocket pilot."

"So what? This is more important."

"I can warn everybody of what's up just as well as two of us can."

"The matter is settled, I tell you."

"Okay. Just wanted to be sure you knew your own mind. Let's go." Jim climbed into his own suit, zipped it up, tightened straps, and then started picking over his belongings. He was forced to throw away a large part, as he wanted Willis to travel in his bag.

He picked up Willis. "Look, fellow," he said, "we're going home. I want you to ride inside here, where it's nice and warm."

"Willis go for ride?"

"Willis go for ride. But I want you to stay inside and not say one word until I take you out. Understand?"

"Willis not talk?"

"Willis not talk at all, not till Jim takes him out."

"Okay, Jim boy." Willis thought about it and added, "Willis play music?"

"No! Not a sound, not a word. No music. Willis close up and stay closed up."

"Okay, Jim boy," Willis answered in aggrieved tones and promptly made a smooth ball of himself. Jim dropped him into the bag and zipped it.

"Come on," said Frank. "Let's find Smitty, get our guns, and get going."

"The Sun won't be up for nearly an hour."

"We'll have to risk it. Say, how much money have you got?"

"Not much. Why?"

"Our fare home, dope."

"Oh—" Jim had been so preoccupied with other matters that he had not thought about the price of a ticket. The trip to the school had been free, of course, but they had no travel authorization for this trip; cash would be required.

They pooled resources—not enough for one ticket, much less than enough for two. "What'll we do?" asked Jim.

"We'll get it out of Smitty."

"How?"

"We'll get it. Let's go."

"Don't forget your ice skates."

Smythe roomed alone, a tribute to his winning personality. When they shook him, he wakened quickly and said, "Very well, officer, I'll go quietly."

"Smitty," said Jim, "we want our—we want those packages."

"I'm closed for the night. Come back in the morning."

"We got to have them *now*."

Smythe got out of bed. "There's an extra charge for night service, of course." He stood on his bunk, removed the grille from his air intake, reached far inside, and hauled out the wrapped guns.

Jim and Frank tore off the wrappings and belted their guns on. Smythe watched them with raised eyebrows. Frank added, "We've got to have some money." He named the amount.

"Why come to me?"

"Because I know you've got it."

"So? And what do I get in return? A sweet smile?"

"No." Frank got out his slide rule, a beautiful circular instrument with twenty-one scales. "How much for that?"

"Mmm—six credits."

"Don't be silly! It cost my father twenty-five."

"Eight, then. I won't be able to get more than ten for it."

"Take it as security for fifteen."

"Ten, cash. I don't run a pawn shop." Jim's slide rule went for a smaller amount, then both their watches, followed by lesser items at lower prices.

At last they had nothing left to sell but their skates, and both boys refused the suggestion although they were still twelve credits short of what they needed. "You've just got to trust us for the rest, Smitty," Frank told him.

Smythe studied the ceiling. "Well, seeing what good customers you've been, I might add that I also collect autographs."

"Huh?"

"I'll have both of yours, on one I.O.U., at six per cent—per month."

"Take it," said Jim.

Finished, they started to leave. Smythe said, "My crystal ball tells me that you gentlemen are about to fade away. How?"

"Just walk out," Jim told him.

"Hmm . . . it does not seem to have come to your attention that the front door is now locked at nights. Our friend and mentor, Mr. Howe, unlocks it himself when he arrives in the morning."

"You're kidding!"

"Go see for yourself."

Frank tugged Jim's arm. "Come on. We'll bust it down if we have to."

"Why do things the hard way?" inquired Smythe. "Go out through the kitchen."

"You mean the back door's not locked?" demanded Frank.

"Oh, it's locked all right."

"Then quit making silly suggestions."

"I should be offended at that," Smythe answered, "but I consider the source. While the back door is locked, it did not occur to brother Howe to install a lock on the garbage dump."

"The *garbage* dump," exploded Jim.

"Take it or leave it. It's your only way to sneak out."

"We'll take it," decided Frank. "Come on, Jim."

"Hold on," put in Smythe. "One of you can operate the dump for the other, but who's going to do it for the second man? He's stuck."

"Oh, I see." Frank looked at him. "You are."

"And what am I offered?"

"Confound you, Smitty, how would you like a lump on the head? You've already taken us for everything but our eye teeth."

Smythe shrugged. "Did I refuse? After all, I told you about it. Very well, I'll chalk it up to overhead—good will, full measure, advertising. Besides, I don't like to see my clients fall afoul the law."

They went quickly to the school's large kitchen. Smythe's cautious progress through the corridors showed long familiarity with casual disregard of rules. Once there, Smythe said, "All right, who goes first?"

Jim eyed the dump with distaste. It was a metal cylinder, barrel-size, laid on its side in the wall. It could be rotated on its main axis by means of a lever set in the wall; a large opening in it permitted refuse to be placed in it from inside the building, then removed from the outside, without disturbing the pressurization of the building—the simplest sort of a pressure lock. The interior showed ample signs of the use for which it was intended. "I'll go first," he volunteered and settled his mask over his face.

"Wait a second," said Frank. He had been eyeing the stocks of canned foods racked around the room. Now he dumped spare clothing from his bag and started replacing it with cans.

"Hurry up," Smythe insisted. "I want to get back to bed before the morning bell rings."

"Yes, why bother?" protested Jim. "We'll be home in a few hours."

"Just a hunch. Okay, I'm ready."

Jim climbed into the dump, drawing up his knees and clutching his bag to his chest. The cylinder rotated around him; he felt a sudden drop in pressure and a bitter cold draft. Then he was picking himself up from the pavement of the alley behind the school.

The cylinder creaked back to the loading position; in a moment Frank landed beside him. Jim helped him up. "Boy, are you a mess!" he said, brushing at a bit of mashed potato that clung to his chum's suit.

"So are you, but there's no time to worry about it. Gee, but it's cold!"

"It'll be warmer soon. Let's go." The pink glow of the coming Sun was already lighting the eastern sky, even though the air was still midnight cold. They hurried down the alley to the street in back of the school and along it to the right. This portion of the city was entirely terrestrial and could have been a city in Alaska or Norway, but beyond them, etched against the lightening sky, were the ancient towers of Syrtis Minor, denying the Earthlike appearance of the street.

They came, as they had planned, to a tributary canal and sat down to put on their skates. They were racers, with 22-inch razorlike blades, intended for speed alone. Jim finished first and lowered himself to the ice. "Better hurry," he said. "I almost froze my behind."

"You're telling me!"

"This ice is almost too hard to take an edge."

Frank joined him; they picked up their bags and set out. A few hundred yards away the little waterway gave into the Grand Canal of the city; they turned into it and made speed for the scooter station. Despite the exercise they were tingling with cold by the time they got to it.

They went through the pressure door and inside. A single clerk was on duty there. He looked up and Frank went to him. "Is there a scooter to South Colony today?"

"In about twenty minutes," said the clerk. "You want to ship those bags?"

"No, we want tickets." Frank handed over their joint funds.

Silently the clerk attended to the transaction. Jim heaved a sigh of relief; scooters to the colony did not run every day. The chance that they might have to keep out of sight for a day or more and then try to get away without encountering Howe had been eating at him.

They took seats in the back of the station and waited. Presently Jim said, "Frank, is Deimos up?"

"I didn't notice. Why?"

"Maybe I can get a call through to home."

"No money."

"I'll put it through collect." He went to the booth opposite the clerk's desk; the clerk looked up but said nothing. Inside, he signalled the operator. Subconsciously he had been worrying about getting word to his father ever since Willis had spilled the secret of the so-called non-migration policy.

The screen lighted up and a pleasant-appearing young woman with the fashionable striped hair appeared therein. "I'd like to call South Colony," he said.

"No relay until later this morning," she informed him. "Would you like to record a delayed message?"

He was stopped; delayed messages were not accepted on a collect basis. "No, thank you, I'll try later," he fibbed and switched off.

The clerk was tapping on the booth's door. "The driver is ready for you," he told Jim. Jim hurriedly settled his mask in place and followed Frank out through the pressure door. The driver was just closing the baggage compartment of the scooter. He took their tickets and the two boys got aboard. Again they were the only passengers; they claimed the observation seats.

Ten minutes later, tired of staring almost into a rising Sun, Jim announced, "I'm sleepy. I think I'll go down."

"I think I'll ask the driver to turn on the radio," said Frank.

"Oh, the heck with that. We've both had a hard night. Come on."

"Well—all right." They went into the lower compartment, found bunks, and crawled in. In a few minutes they both were snoring.

The scooter, leaving Syrtis Minor at sunrise, kept ahead of the daily thaw and did not have to lay over at Hesperidum. It continued south and reached Cynia about noon. So far advanced was the season that there was no worry about the ice holding from Cynia south to Charax; Strymon canal would not thaw again until the following spring.

The driver was pleased to have kept his schedule. When Deimos rose toward the end of the morning's run he relaxed and switched on his radio. What he heard caused him to make a quick check of his passengers. They were still asleep; he decided not to do anything about it until he reached Cynia Station.

On reaching there he hurried inside. Jim and Frank were awakened by the scooter stopping but did not get out. Presently the driver came back and said, "Meal stop. Everybody out."

Frank answered, "We're not hungry."

The driver looked disconcerted. "Better, come in anyhow," he insisted. "It gets pretty cold in the car when she's standing still."

"We don't mind." Frank was thinking that he would dig a can of something out of his bag as soon as the driver had left; from suppertime the night before until noon today seemed a long time to his stomach.

"What's the trouble?" the driver continued. "Broke?" Something in their expressions caused him to continue, "I'll stake you to a sandwich each."

Frank refused but Jim interceded. "Don't be silly, Frank. Thank you, sir. We accept."

George, the agent and factotum of Cynia station, looked at them speculatively and served them sandwiches without comment. The driver bolted his food and was quickly through. When he got up, the boys did so, too. "Just take it easy," he advised them. "I've got twenty, thirty minutes' work, loading and checking."

"Can't we help you?" asked Jim.

"Nope. You'd just be in the way. I'll call you when I'm ready."

"Well—thanks for the sandwich."

"Don't mention it." He went out.

Less than ten minutes later there came faintly to their ears the sound of the scooter starting up. Frank looked startled and rushed to the traffic-checking window. The car was already disappearing to the south. Frank turned to the agent. "Hey, he didn't wait for us!"

"Nope."

"But he said he'd call us."

"Yep." The agent resumed reading.

"But—but *why*," insisted Frank. "He told us to wait."

The agent put down his newspaper. "It's like this," he said, "Clem is a peaceable man and he told me that he wasn't a cop. He said he would have no part in trying to arrest two strapping, able-bodied boys, both wearing guns."

"*What!*"

"That's what I said. And don't go to fiddling around with

those heaters. You'll notice I ain't wearing my gun; you can take the station apart for all of me."

Jim had joined Frank at the counter. "What's this all about?" he asked.

"You tell me. All I know is, there's a call out to pick you up. You're charged with burglary, theft, truancy, destruction of company property—pretty near everything. Seems like you are a couple of desperate characters—though you don't look the part."

"I see," said Frank slowly. "Well, what are you going to do about it?"

"Nothing. Nothing at all. 'Long about tomorrow morning a special scooter will arrive and I presume there will be force enough aboard her to subdue a couple of outlaws. In the meantime do as you please. Go outside. Wander around. When you get chilly, come back inside." He went back to his reading.

"I see. Come along, Jim." They retreated to the far corner of the room for a war conference. The agent's attitude was easily understood. Cynia station was almost literally a thousand miles from anywhere; the station itself was the only human habitation against the deadly cold of night.

Jim was almost in tears. "I'm sorry, Frank. If I hadn't been so darned anxious to eat, this wouldn't have happened."

"Don't be so tragic about it," Frank advised him. "Can you imagine us shooting it out with a couple of innocent bystanders and hijacking the scooter? I can't."

"Uh—no. I guess you're right."

"Certainly I am. What we've got to decide is what to do next."

"I know one thing; I'm not going to let them drag me back to school."

"Neither am I. What's more important, we've got to get word to our folks about the deal that's being cooked up against them."

"Say, look—maybe we can phone now!"

"Do you think he"—Frank nodded toward the agent—"would let us?"

"Maybe. Maybe not. We've still got our guns—and I can

be pushed just so far." Jim got up and went to the agent. "Any objection to us using the phone?"

The agent did not even glance up. "Not a bit. Help yourself."

Jim went into the booth. There was no local exchange; the instrument was simply a radio link to the relay station on the outer moon. A transparency announced that Deimos was above the horizon; seeing this, Jim punched the call button and asked for linkage to South Colony.

There was an unusually long delay, then a sweetly impersonal voice announced, "Due to circumstances beyond our control calls are not being accepted from Cynia station to South Colony."

Jim started to ask if Deimos were visible at South Colony, since he knew that line-of-sight was essential to radio transmission on Mars—indeed, it was the only sort of radio transmission he was familiar with—but the relay station had switched off and made no answer when he again punched the call button. He left the booth and told Frank about it.

"Sounds like Howe has fixed us," Frank commented. "I don't believe there is a breakdown. Unless——"

"Unless what?"

"Unless there is more to it than that. Beecher may be rigging things to interfere with messages getting through until he's put over his scheme."

"Frank, we've got to get word to our folks. See here, I bet we could hole up with the Martians over at Cynia. After all, they offered us water and——"

"Suppose we could. Where does that get us?"

"Let me finish. We can mail a letter from here, giving our folks all the details and telling them where we are hiding. Then we could wait for them to come and get us."

Frank shook his head. "If we mail a letter from here, old frozen face over there is bound to know it. Then, when the cops show up and we are gone, he turns it over to them. Instead of our folks getting it, it goes back to Howe and Beecher."

"You really think so? Nobody has any right to touch private mail."

"Don't be a little innocent. Howe didn't have any right to order us to give up our guns—but he did. No, Jim, we've got to carry this message ourselves."

On the wall opposite them was a map of the area served by Cynia station. Frank had been studying it idly while they talked. Suddenly he said, "Jim, what's that new station south of Cynia?"

"Huh? Where do you mean?"

"There." Frank pointed. Inked on the original map was a station on west Strymon, south of them.

"That?" said Jim. "That must be one of the shelters for the Project." The grand plan for restoring oxygen to Mars called for setting up, the following spring, a string of processing plants in the desert between Cynia and Charax. Some of the shelters had already been completed in anticipation of the success of atmosphere plant number one in Libya.

"It can't be much over a hundred miles away."

"A hundred and ten, maybe," Jim commented, looking at the scale.

Frank got a far-away look in his eyes. "I think I can skate that far before dark. Are you game?"

"What? Are you crazy? We'd still be better than seven hundred miles from home."

"We can skate better than two hundred miles a day," answered Frank. "Aren't there more shelters?"

"The map doesn't show any." Jim thought. "I *know* they've finished more than one; I've heard Dad talking about it."

"If we had to, we could skate all night and sleep in the day time. That way we wouldn't freeze."

"Hmm . . . I think you're kidding yourself. I saw a man once who was caught out at night. He was stiff as a board. All right, when do we start?"

"Right now."

They picked up their bags and headed for the door. The agent looked up and said, "Going somewhere?"

"For a walk."

"Might as well leave your bags. You'll be back."

They did not answer but went on out the door. Five minutes later they were skating south on west Strymon.

"Hey, Jim!"

"What?"

"Let's stop for a minute. I want to sling my bag."

"Just what I was thinking." Their travel bags unbalanced them and prevented proper arm motion and any real speed. But skating was a common form of locomotion; the bags had straps which permitted them to be slung as haversacks. Jim opened his before he put it on; Willis extended his eye stalks and looked at him reproachfully. "Jim boy gone long time."

"Sorry, old fellow."

"Willis not talk."

"Willis can talk all he wants to now. Look, if I leave the bag open a little bit so that you can see, will you manage not to fall out?"

"Willis want out."

"Can't do that; I'm going to take you for a fine ride. You won't fall out?"

"Willis not fall out."

"Okay." He slung the bag and they set out again.

They picked up speed. With fast ice, little air resistance, and the low Martian gravity the speed of a skater on Mars is limited by his skill in stroking. Both of the boys were able. Willis let out a "Wheel" and they settled down to putting miles behind them.

The desert plateau between Cynia and Charax is higher than the dead sea bottom between Cynia and the equator. This drop is used to move the waters of the southern polar cap across the desert to the great green belt near the equator. In midwinter the southern ice cap reaches to Charax; the double canal of Strymon, which starts at Charax, is one of the principal discharge points for the polar cap when it melts in the spring.

The boys were starting at the lower end of the canal's drop; the walls of the canal reached high above their heads. Furthermore the water level—or ice level—was low because the season was late autumn; the water level would be much higher during spring flood. There was nothing to see but the banks of the canal converging ahead of them, the blue sky beyond, and the purple-black sky overhead. The Sun was behind them and a bit west of meridian; it was moving north toward northern summer solstice. Seasons do not lag on Mars as much as they do on Earth; there are no oceans to hold the heat and the only "flywheel" of the climate is the freezing and melting of the polar caps.

With nothing to see the boys concentrated on skating, heads down and shoulders swinging.

After many miles of monotonous speed Jim grew careless; the toe of his right runner caught on some minor obstruction in the ice. He went down. His suit saved him from ice burns and he knew how to fall safely, but Willis popped out of his bag like a cork from a bottle.

The bouncer, true to instinct, hauled in all excrescences at once. He hit as a ball and rolled; he traveled over the ice for several hundred yards. Frank threw himself into a hockey stop as soon as he saw Jim tumble. He stopped in a shower of ice particles and went back to help Jim up. "You all right?"

"Sure. Where's Willis?"

They skated on and recovered the bouncer who was now standing on his tiny legs and waiting for them. "Whoopee!" yelled Willis as they came up. "Do it again!"

"Not if I can help it," Jim assured him and stuffed him back in the bag. "Say, Frank, how long have we been traveling?"

"Not over three hours," Frank decided, after a glance at the Sun.

"I wish I had my watch," complained Jim. "We don't want to overrun the shelter."

"Oh, we won't come to it for another couple of hours, at least."

"But what's to keep us from passing right by it? We can't see over these banks."

"Want to turn around and go back?"

"No."

"Then quit worrying."

Jim shut up but continued to worry. Perhaps that was why

he noticed the only indication of the shelter when they came to it, for Frank skated on past it. It was merely a ramp down the bank. There were such ramps every few miles, as ancient as the canals themselves, but this one had set above it an overhanging beam, as if to support a hoist. Jim spotted it as terrestrial workmanship.

He stopped. Frank skated on ahead, noticed presently that Jim was not following him and came back. "What's up?" he called out.

"I think this is it."

"Hmm . . . could be." They removed their skates and climbed the ramp. At the top, set back a short distance from the bank, was one of the bubble-shaped buildings which are the sign anywhere on Mars of the alien from Earth. Beyond it a foundation had been started for the reducing plant. Jim heaved a big sigh. Frank nodded and said, "Just about where we expected to find it."

"And none too soon," added Jim. The Sun was close to the western horizon and dropping closer as they watched.

There was, of course, no one in the shelter; no further work would be done at this latitude until the following spring. The shelter was unpressurized; they simply unlatched the outer door, walked through the inner door without delay. Frank groped for the light switch, found it, and lighted up the place—the lighting circuit was powered by the building's atomic-fuel power pack and did not require the presence of men.

It was a simple shelter, lined with bunks except for the space occupied by the kitchen unit. Frank looked around happily. "Looks like we've found a home from home, Jim."

"Yep." Jim looked around, located the shelter's thermostat, and cut it in. Shortly the room became warmer and with it there was a soft sighing sound as the building's pressure regulator, hooked in with the thermostat, started the building's supercharger. In a few minutes the boys were able to remove their masks and finally their outdoors suits as well.

Jim poked around the kitchen unit, opening cupboards and peering into shelves. "Find anything?" asked Frank.

"Nary a thing. Seems like they could have left at least a can of beans."

"Now maybe you're glad I raided the kitchen before we left. Supper in five minutes."

"Okay, so you've got a real talent for crime," acknowledged Jim. "I salute you." He tried the water tap. "Plenty of water in the tanks," he announced.

"Good!" Frank answered. "That saves me having to go down and chip ice. I need to fill my mask. I was dry the last few miles." The high coxcomb structure on a Mars mask is not only a little supercharger with its power pack, needed to pressurize the mask; it is also a small water reservoir. A nipple in the mask permits the wearer to take a drink outdoors, but this is a secondary function. The prime need for water in a Mars mask is to wet a wick through which the air is forced before it reaches the wearer's nose.

"You were? Don't you know better than to drink yourself dry?"

"I forgot to fill it before we left."

"Tourist!"

"Well, we left in kind of a hurry, you know."

"How long were you dry?"

"I don't know exactly," Frank evaded.

"How's your throat?"

"All right. A little dry, maybe."

"Let me see it," Jim persisted, coming closer.

Frank pushed him away. "I tell you it's all right. Let's eat."

"Well—okay."

They dined off canned corned beef hash and went promptly to bed. Willis snuggled up against Jim's stomach and imitated his snores.

Breakfast was more of the same, since there was some hash left and Frank insisted that they not waste anything. Willis had no breakfast since he had eaten only two weeks before, but he absorbed nearly a quart of water. As they were about to leave Jim held up a flashlight. "Look what I found."

"Well, put it back and let's go."

"I think I'll keep it," Jim answered, stuffing it in his bag. "We might have a use for it."

"We won't and it's not yours."

"For criminy's sake, I'm not swiping it; I'm just borrowing it. This is an emergency."

Frank shrugged. "Okay, let's get moving." A few minutes later they were on the ice and again headed south. It was a beautiful day, as Martian days almost always are; when the Sun was high enough to fill the slot of the canal it was almost balmy, despite the late season. Frank spotted the tell-tale hoisting beam of a Project shelter around midday and they were able to lunch inside, which saved them the tedious, messy, and unsatisfactory chore of trying to eat through the mouth valve of a respirator mask. The shelter was a twin of the first but no foundation for the plant had as yet been built near it.

As they were preparing to leave the shelter Jim said, "You look sort of flushed, Frank. Got a fever?"

"That's just the bloom of health," Frank insisted. "I'm fine." Nevertheless he coughed as he put on his mask. "Mars throat," Jim thought but said nothing as there was nothing that he could do for Frank.

Mars throat is not a disease in itself; it is simply an extremely dry condition of the nose and throat which arises from direct exposure to Martian air. The humidity on Mars is usually effectively zero; a throat dehydrated by it is wide open to whatever disease organisms there may be present in the human throat at the time. The result is usually a virulent sore throat.

The afternoon passed without incident. As the Sun began to drop toward the skyline it seemed possible that home was not much more than five hundred miles away. Jim had watched Frank closely all afternoon. His chum seemed to be skating as strongly as ever; perhaps, he decided, the cough was just a false alarm. He skated up alongside Frank. "I guess we had better start watching for a shelter."

"Suits me."

Soon they passed another of the ramps built by long-dead Martians, but there was no hoisting beam above it nor any other sign of terrestrial activity. The banks, though somewhat lower now, were still too high to see over. Jim stepped up the stroke a bit; they hurried on.

They came to another ramp, but again there was nothing to suggest that a shelter might be above it. Jim stopped. "I vote we take a look up the bank," he said. "We *know* they build the shelters by the ramps and they may have taken the hoist down for some reason."

"It would just be wasting valuable time," Frank protested. "If we hurry, we can get to another ramp before dark."

"Well, if you say so—" Jim shoved off and picked up speed.

The next ramp was the same story; Jim stopped again. "Let's take a look," he pleaded. "We can't possibly reach the next one before sundown."

"Okay." Frank stooped over and tugged at his skates.

They hurried up the bank and reached the top. The slanting rays of the Sun showed nothing but the vegetation bordering the canal.

Jim felt ready to bawl through sheer weariness and disappointment. "Well, what do we do now?" he said.

"We go back down," Frank answered, "and keep going until we find it."

"I don't think we could spot one of those hoist beams in the dark."

"Then we keep going," Frank said grimly, "until we fall flat on our faces."

"More likely we'll freeze."

"Well, if you want my opinion," Frank replied, "I think we're washed up. I, for one, can't keep going all night, even if we don't freeze."

"You don't feel good?"

"That's putting it mildly. Come on."

"All right."

Willis had climbed out of the bag and up on Jim's shoulder, in order to see better. Now he bounced to the ground and rolled away. Jim snatched at him and missed. "Hey! Willis! Come back here!"

Willis did not answer. Jim started after him. His progress

was difficult. Ordinarily he would have gone under the canal plants, but, late in the day as it was, most of them had lowered almost to knee height preparatory to withdrawing into the ground for the night. Some of the less hardy plants were already out of sight, leaving bare patches of ground.

The vegetation did not seem to slow up Willis but Jim found it troublesome; he could not catch the little scamp. Frank shouted, " 'Ware water-seekers! Watch where you put your feet!" Thus warned, Jim proceeded more carefully—and still more slowly. He stopped. "Willis! Oh, Willis! Come back! Come back, doggone it, or we'll go away and leave you." It was a completely empty threat.

Frank came crashing up and joined him. "We can't hang around up here, Jim."

"I know it. Wouldn't you know that he would pull a stunt like this just at the wrong time?"

"He's a pest, that's what he is. Come on."

Willis's voice—or, rather, Jim's voice as used by Willis—reached them from a distance. "Jim boy! Jim! Come here!"

Jim struggled through the shrinking vegetation with Frank after him. They found the bouncer resting at the edge of an enormous plant, a desert cabbage quite fifty yards across. The desert cabbage is not often found near the canals; it is a weed and not tolerated in the green sea bottoms of the lower latitudes, though it may be found in the desert miles from any surface water.

The western half of this specimen was still spread out in a semi-circular fan, flat to the ground, but the eastern half was tilted up almost vertically, its flat leaves still reaching greedily for the Sun's rays to fuel the photosynthesis by which plants live. A hardy plant, it would not curl up until the Sun was gone completely, and it would not withdraw into the ground at all. Instead it would curl into a tight ball, thus protecting itself from the cold and incidentally simulating, on giant scale, the Earth plant for which it was named.

Willis sat by the edge of the half that was flat to the ground. Jim reached for him.

Willis bounced up on the edge of the desert cabbage and rolled toward the heart of the plant. Jim stopped and said, "Oh, Willis, darn your eyes, come back here. Please come back."

"Don't go after him," warned Frank. "That thing might close up on you. The Sun is almost down."

"I won't. Willis! Come back!"

Willis called back, "Come here, Jim boy."

"*You* come *here*."

"Jim boy come here. Frank come here. Cold there. Warm here."

"Frank, what'll I do?"

Willis called again. "Come, Jim boy. Warm! Stay warm all night."

Jim stared. "You know what, Frank? I think he means to let it close up on him. And he wants us to join him."

"Sounds that way."

"Come, Jim! Come, Frank!" Willis insisted. "Hurry!"

"Maybe he knows what he's doing," Frank added. "Like Doc says, he's got instincts for Mars and we haven't."

"But we can't go inside a cabbage. It would crush us."

"I wonder."

"Anyhow, we'd suffocate."

"Probably." Frank suddenly added. "Do as you like, Jim. I can't skate any farther." He set foot on a broad leaf—which flinched under the contact—and strode steadily toward the bouncer. Jim watched for a moment and then ran after them.

Willis greeted them ecstatically. "Good boy, Frank! Good boy, Jim! Stay nice and warm all night."

The Sun was slipping behind a distant dune; the sunset wind whipped coldly at them. The far edges of the plant lifted and began to curl toward them. "We still could get out if we jumped, Frank," Jim said nervously.

"I'm staying." Nevertheless Frank eyed the approaching leaves apprehensively.

"We'll smother."

"Maybe. That's better than freezing."

The inner leaves were beginning to curl faster than the outer leaves. Such a leaf, four feet wide at its widest and at least ten feet long, raised up back of Jim and curved in until it touched his shoulder. Nervously he struck at it. The leaf snatched itself away, then slowly resumed its steady progress toward him. "Frank," Jim said shrilly, "they'll smother us!"

Frank looked apprehensively at the broad leaves, now curling up all around them. "Jim," he said, "sit down. Spread your legs wide. Then take my hands and make an arch."

"What for?"

"So that we'll take up as much space as possible. Hurry!"

Jim hurried. With elbows and knees and hands the two managed to occupy a roughly spherical space about five feet across and a little less than that high. The leaves closed down on them, seemed to feel them out, then settled firmly against them, but not, however, with sufficient pressure to crush them. Soon the last open space was covered and they were in total darkness. "Frank," Jim demanded, "we can move now, can't we?"

"No! Give the outside leaves a chance to settle into place."

Jim kept still for quite a long while. He knew that considerable time had passed for he spent the time counting up to one thousand. He was just starting on his second thousand when Willis stirred in the space between his legs. "Jim boy, Frank boy—nice and warm, huh?"

"Yeah, Willis," he agreed. "Say, how about it, Frank?"

"I think we can relax now." Frank lowered his arms; the inner leaf forming the ceiling immediately above him at once curled down and brushed him in the dark. He slapped at it instinctively; it retreated.

Jim said, "It's getting stuffy already."

"Don't worry about it. Take it easy. Breathe shallowly. Don't talk and don't move and you'll use up less oxygen."

"What difference does it make whether we suffocate in ten minutes or an hour? This was a crazy thing to do, Frank; any way you figure it we can't last till morning."

"Why can't we? I read in a book that back in India men have let themselves be buried alive for days and even weeks and were still alive when they were dug up. Fakirs, they called them."

" 'Fakers' is right! I don't believe it."

"I read it in a book, I tell you."

"I suppose you think that anything that's printed in a book is true?"

Frank hesitated before replying, "It had better be true because it's the only chance we've got. Now will you shut up? If you keep yapping, you'll use up what air there is and kill us both off and it'll be your fault."

Jim shut up. All that he could hear was Frank's breathing. He reached down and touched Willis; the bouncer had withdrawn all his stalks. He was a smooth ball, apparently asleep. Presently Frank's breathing changed to rasping snores.

Jim tried to sleep but could not. The utter darkness and the increasing deadness of the air pressed down on him like a great weight. He wished again for his watch, lost to Smythe's business talent; if he only knew what time it was, how long it was until sunrise, he felt that he could stand it.

He became convinced that the night had passed—or had almost passed. He began to expect the dawn and with it the unrolling of the giant plant. When he had been expecting it "any minute now" for a time that he estimated at two hours, at least, he became panicky. He knew how late in the season it was; he knew also that desert cabbages hibernated by the simple method of remaining closed through the winter. Apparently Frank and he had had the enormous bad luck to take shelter in a cabbage on the very night on which it started its hibernation.

Twelve long months from now, more than three hundred days in the future, the plant would open to the spring Sun and release them—dead. He was sure of it.

He remembered the flashlight he had picked up in the first Project shelter. The thought of it stimulated him, took his mind off his fears for the moment. He leaned forward, twisted around and tried to get at his bag, still strapped to his shoulders.

The leaves above him closed in; he struck at them and

they shrank away. He was able to reach the torch, drag it out, and turn it on. Its rays brightly illuminated the cramped space. Frank stopped snoring, blinked, and said, "What's the matter?"

"I just remembered this. Good thing I brought it, huh?"

"Better put it out and go to sleep."

"It doesn't use up any oxygen. I feel better with it on."

"Maybe you do, but as long as you stay awake *you* use up more oxygen."

"I suppose so." Jim suddenly recalled what had been terrifying him before he got out the light. "It doesn't make any difference." He explained to Frank his conviction that they were trapped forever in the plant.

"Nonsense!" said Frank.

"Nonsense yourself! Why didn't it open up at dawn?"

"Because," Frank said, "we haven't been in here more than an hour."

"What?"

"Not more than an hour. Now shut up and let me sleep. Better put out that light." Frank settled his head again on his knees.

Jim shut up but did not turn out the light. It comforted him. Besides, the inner leaves which had shown an annoying tendency to close in on the tops of their heads now had retreated and flattened themselves firmly against the dense wall formed by the outer layers of leaves. Under the mindless reflex which controlled the movements of the plant they were doing their best to present maximum surface to the rays from the flashlight.

Jim did not analyze the matter; his knowledge of photosynthesis and of heliotropism was sketchy. He was simply aware that the place seemed roomier in the light and that he was having less trouble with the clinging leaves. He settled the torch against Willis, who had not stirred, and tried to relax.

It actually seemed less stuffy with the light on. He had the impression that the pressure was up a little. He considered trying to take off his mask but decided against it. Presently, without knowing it, he drifted off to sleep.

He dreamed and then dreamt that he was dreaming. Hiding in the desert cabbage had been only a fantastic, impossible dream, school and Headmaster Howe had merely been nightmares; he was home, asleep in his bed, with Willis cuddled against him. Tomorrow Frank and he would start for Syrtis Minor to enter school.

It had simply been a nightmare, caused by the suggestion that Willis be taken away from him. They were planning to take Willis away from him! They couldn't do that; he wouldn't let them!

Again his dream shifted; again he defied Headmaster Howe; again he rescued Willis and fled—and again they were locked away in the heart of a desert plant.

He knew with bitter certainty that it would always end like this. This was the reality, to be trapped and smothering in the core of a hibernating giant weed—to die there.

He choked and muttered, tried to wake up, then slipped into a less intolerable dream.

VII

PURSUED

TINY PHOBOS, inner moon of Mars, came out of eclipse and, at breakneck speed, flew west to east into the face of the rising Sun. The leisurely spin of its ruddy primary, twenty-four and a half hours for each rotation, presently brought the rays of that Sun to east Strymon, then across the band of desert between the twin canals and to the banks of west Strymon. The rays struck a great ball perched near the eastern bank of that canal, a desert cabbage closed against the cold.

The plant stirred and unfolded. The sunward half of the plant opened flat to the ground; the other half fanned itself open like a spread peacock's tail to catch the almost horizontal rays. In so doing it spilled something out of its heart and onto the flat portion—two human bodies, twisted and stiff, clad garishly in elastic suits and grotesque helmets.

A tiny ball spilled out with them, rolled a few yards over the thick green leaves, and stopped. It extended eye stalks and little bumps of legs and waddled back to the sprawled bodies. It nuzzled up against one.

It hesitated, nuzzled again, then settled back and let out a thin wailing in which was compounded inconsolable grief and an utter sense of loss.

Jim opened one bloodshot eye. "Cut out that infernal racket," he said crossly.

Willis shrieked, "Jim boy!" and jumped upon his stomach, where he continued to bounce up and down in an ecstasy of greeting.

Jim brushed him off, then gathered him up in one arm. "Calm down. Behave yourself. Ouch!"

"What's the matter, Jim boy?"

"My arm's stiff. Ooo—ouch!" Further efforts had shown Jim that his legs were stiff as well. Also his back. And his neck.

"What's the matter with you?" demanded Frank.

"Stiff as board. I'd do better to skate on my hands today. Say——"

"Say what?"

"Maybe we don't skate. I wonder if the spring floods have started?"

"Huh? What are you gibbering about?" Frank sat up, slowly and carefully.

"Why, the spring floods, of course. Somehow we lasted through the winter, though I don't know how. Now we——"

"Don't be any sillier than you have to be. Look where the Sun is rising."

Jim looked. Martian colonials are more acutely aware of the apparent movements of the Sun than any Earthbound men, except, possibly, the Eskimos. All he said was, "Oh . . ." then added, "I guess it was a dream."

"Either that or you are even nuttier than usual. Let's get going." Frank struggled to his feet with a groan.

"How do you feel?"

"Like my own grandfather."

"I mean, how's your throat?" Jim persisted.

"Oh, it's all right." Frank promptly contradicted himself by a fit of coughing. By great effort he controlled it shortly; coughing while wearing a respirator is a bad idea. Sneezing is worse.

"Want some breakfast?"

"I'm not hungry now," Frank answered. "Let's find a shelter first, so we can eat in comfort."

"Okay." Jim stuffed Willis back into the bag; discovered by experiment that he could stand and walk. Noticing the flashlight, he tucked it in with Willis and followed Frank toward the bank. The canal vegetation was beginning to show; even as they walked the footing grew more tangled. The green plants, still stiff with night cold, could not draw away quickly as they brushed through them.

They reached the bank. "The ramp must be about a hundred yards off to the right," Frank decided. "Yep—I see it. Come on."

Jim grabbed his arm and drew him back. " 'Smatter?" demanded Frank.

"Look on up the canal, north."

"Huh? Oh!" A scooter was proceeding toward them. Instead of the two hundred fifty miles per hour or more that such craft usually make, this one throttled down to a minimum. Two men were seated on top of it, out in the open.

Frank drew back hastily. "Good boy, Jim," he approved. "I was just about to walk right into them. I guess we had better let them get well ahead."

"Willis good boy, too," Willis put in smugly.

"Let them get ahead, my foot!" Jim answered. "Can't you see what they're doing?"

"Huh?"

They're following our tracks!

Frank looked startled but did not answer. He peered cautiously out. "Look out!" Jim snapped. "He's got binoculars."

Frank ducked back. But he had seen enough; the scooter had stopped at approximately the spot where they had stopped the night before. One of the men on top was gesturing through the observation dome at the driver and pointing to the ramp.

Canal ice was, of course, never cleaned of skate marks; the surface was renewed from time to time by midday thaws until the dead freeze of winter set in. However, it was unlikely that anyone but the two boys had skated over this stretch of ice, so far from any settlement, any time in months. The ice held scooter tracks, to be sure, but, like all skaters, Jim and Frank had avoided them in favor of untouched ice.

Now their unmistakable spoor lay for any to read from Cynia station to the ramp near them.

"If we head back into the bushes," Jim whispered. "We can hide until they go away. They'll never find us in this stuff."

"Suppose they don't go away. Do you want to spend another night in the cabbage?"

"They're bound to go away eventually."

"Sure but not soon enough. They know we went up the ramp; they'll stay and they'll search, longer than we can hold out. They can afford to; they've got a base."

"Well, what do we do?"

"We head south along the bank, on foot, at least as far as the next ramp."

"Let's get going, then. They'll be up the ramp in no time."

With Frank in the lead they dog-trotted to the south. The plants along the bank were high enough now to permit them to go under; Frank held a course about thirty feet in from the bank. The gloom under the spreading leaves and the stems of the plants themselves protected them from any distant observation.

Jim kept an eye out for snake worms and water-seekers and cautioned Willis to do likewise. They made fair time. After a few minutes Frank stopped, motioned for silence, and they both listened. All that Jim could hear was Frank's rasping breath; if they were being pursued, the pursuers were not close.

They were at least two miles south of the ramp when Frank stopped very suddenly. Jim bumped into him and the two almost tumbled into the thing that had caused Frank to stop—another canal. This one ran east and west and was a much narrower branch of the main canal. There were several such between Cynia and Charax. Some of them joined the east and west legs of Strymon canal; some merely carried water to local depressions in the desert plateau.

Jim stared down into the deep and narrow gash. "For the love of Mike! We nearly took a header."

Frank did not answer. He sank down to his knees, then sat and held his head. Suddenly he was overcome by a spasm of coughing. When it was over, his shoulder still shook, as if he were racked by dry sobs.

Jim put a hand on his arm. "You're pretty sick, aren't you, fellow?"

Frank did not answer. Willis said, "Poor Frank boy," and tut-tutted.

Jim stared again at the canal, his forehead wrinkled. Presently Frank raised his head and said, "I'm all right. It just got me for a moment—running into the canal and all and realizing it had us stopped. I was so tired."

Jim said, "Look here, Frank, I've got a new plan. I'm going to follow this ditch off to the east until I find some way to get down into it. You're going to go back and give yourself up——"

"No!"

"Wait till I finish! This makes sense. You're too sick to keep going. If you stay out here, you're going to die. You might as well admit it. Somebody's got to get the word to our folks—me. You go back, surrender, and then give them a song and dance about how I went that way—any way but this way. If you make it good, you can stall them and keep them chasing their tails for a full day and give me that much headstart. In the mean time you lie around in the scooter, warm and safe, and tonight you're in bed in the infirmary at school. There—doesn't that make sense?"

"No."

"Why not? You're just being stubborn."

"No," repeated Frank, "it's no good. In the first place I won't turn myself over to them. I'd rather die out here——"

"Nuts!"

"Nuts yourself. In the second place, a day's start will do you no good. Once they are sure you aren't where I say you are, they'll just go back to combing the canal, by scooter. They'll pick you up tomorrow."

"But—well, what is the answer then?"

"I don't know, but it's not that." He was seized again by coughing.

Neither one of them said anything for several minutes. At last Jim said, "What kind of a scooter was that?"

"The usual cargo sort, a Hudson Six Hundred I think. Why?"

"Could it turn around on that ice down there?"

Frank looked down into the small canal. Its sides sloped in toward the bottom; the water level was so low that the ice surface was barely twenty feet across. "Not a chance," he answered.

"Then they won't try to search this branch by scooter—at least not in *that* scooter."

"I'm way ahead of you," put in Frank. "You figure we'll cross to east Strymon and go home that way. But how do you know this cut runs all the way through? You remember the map that well?"

"No, I don't. But there is a good chance it does. If it doesn't, it will run most of the way across and we'll just have to hoof it the rest of the way."

"After we get to the east leg it will still be five hundred miles or so to Charax. This leg has shelters on it, even if we did miss the one last night."

"We've got just as good a chance of finding project shelters on east leg as on west leg," Jim answered. "The Project starts next spring on both sides. I know—Dad's talked about it enough. Anyhow, we can't use this leg any further; they're searching it—so why beat your choppers about it? The real question is: can you skate? If you can't, I still say you ought to surrender."

Frank stood up. "I'll skate," he said grimly. "Come on."

They went boldly along the stone embankment, convinced that their pursuers were still searching the neighborhood of the ramp. They were three or four miles further east when they came to a ramp leading down to the ice. "Shall we chance it?" asked Jim.

"Sure. Even if they send a man in on skates I doubt if he would come this far with no tracks to lead him on. I'm tired of walking." They went down, put on their skates, and started. Most of the kinks from their uncomfortable night had been smoothed out by walking; it felt good to be on the ice again. Jim let Frank set the pace; despite his illness he stroked right into it and pushed the miles behind them.

They had come perhaps forty miles when the banks began to be noticeably lower. Jim, seeing this, got a sick feeling that the little canal was not cross-connecting from west to east leg, but merely a feeder to a low spot in the desert. He kept his suspicion to himself. At the end of the next hour it was no longer necessary to spare his chum; the truth was evident to them both. The banks were now so low that they could see over them and the ice ahead no longer disappeared into the blue sky but dead-ended in some fashion.

They came to the dead end presently, a frozen swamp. The banks were gone; the rough ice spread out in all directions and was bordered in the distance by green plants. Here and there, canal grass, caught by the freeze, stuck up in dead tufts through the ice.

They continued east, skating where they could and picking their way around bits of higher ground. At last Frank said, "All out! End of the line!" and sat down to take off his skates.

"I'm sorry, Frank."

"About what? We'll leg it the rest of the way. It can't be so many miles."

They set out through the surrounding greenery, walking

99

just fast enough to let the plants draw out of their way. The vegetation that surrounded the marsh was lower than the canal plants, hardly shoulder high, and showed smaller leaves. After a couple of miles of this they found themselves out on the sand dunes.

The shifting, red, iron-oxide sands made hard walking and the dunes, to be climbed or skirted, made it worse. Jim usually elected to climb them even if Frank went around; he was looking for a dark green line against the horizon that would mark east Strymon. It continued to disappoint him.

Willis insisted on getting down. First he gave himself a dust bath in the clean sand; thereafter he kept somewhat ahead of Jim, exploring this way and that and startling the spin bugs. Jim had just topped a dune and was starting down the other side when he heard an agonized squeak from Willis. He looked around.

Frank was just coming around the end of the dune and Willis was with him, that is to say, Willis had skittered on ahead. Now the bouncer was standing dead still. Frank apparently had noticed nothing; he was dragging along in a listless fashion, his head down.

Charging straight at them was a water-seeker.

It was a long shot, even for a match marksman. The scene took on a curious unreality to Jim. It seemed as if Frank were frozen in his tracks and as if the water-seeker itself were strolling slowly toward his victims. Jim himself seemed to have all the time in the world to draw, take a steady, careful bead, and let go his first charge.

It burned the creature, but it kept coming.

Jim sighted on it again, held the stud down. His beam, held steadily on the centerline of the varmit, sliced it in two as if it had run into a buzz saw. It kept coming until its two halves were no longer joined, until they fell two ways, twitching. The great scimitar claw on the left half stopped within inches of Willis.

Jim ran down the dune. Frank, no longer a statue, actually had stopped. He was standing, blinking at what had been a moment before the incarnation of sudden and bloody death. He looked around as Jim came up. "Thanks," he said.

Jim did not answer but kicked at a trembling leg of the beast. "The filthy thing!" he said intensely. "Gosh, how I hate them. I wish I could burn every one on Mars, all at once." He walked on up along the body, located the egg sac, and carefully blasted every bit of it.

Willis had not moved. He was sobbing quietly. Jim came back, picked him up, and popped him into the travel bag. "Let's stick together from here on," he said. "If you don't feel like climbing, I'll go around."

"Okay."

"Frank!"

"Uh? Yes, what is it, Jim?" Frank's voice was listless.

"What do you see ahead?"

"Ahead?" Frank tried manfully to make his eyes focus, to chase the fuzz from them. "Uh, it's the canal, the green belt I mean. I guess we made it."

"And what else? Don't you see a tower?"

"What? Where? Oh, there— Yes, I guess I do. It's a tower all right."

"Well, for heaven's sake, don't you know what that means? Martians!"

"Yeah, I suppose so."

"Well, show some enthusiasm!"

"Why should I?"

"They'll take us in, man! Martians are good people; you'll have a warm place to rest, before we go on."

Frank looked a bit more interested, but said nothing. "They might even know Gekko," Jim went on. "This is a real break."

"Maybe so."

It took another hour of foot-slogging before the little Martian town was reached. It was so small that it boasted only one tower, but to Jim it was even more beautiful than Syrtis Major. They followed its wall and presently found a gate.

They had not been inside more than a few minutes when Jim's hopes, so high, were almost as low as they could be. Even before he saw the weed-choked central garden, the empty walks and silent courts had told him the bad truth: the little town was deserted.

Mars must once have held a larger native population than it does today. Ghost cities are not unknown and even the greater centers of population, such as Charax, Syrtis Major and Minor, and Hesperidum, have areas which are no longer used and through which tourists from Earth may sometimes be conducted. This little town, apparently never of great importance, might have been abandoned before Noah laid the keel of his ship.

Jim paused in the plaza, unwilling to speak. Frank stopped and sat down on a metal slab, its burnished face bright with characters that an Earthly scholar would have given an arm to read. "Well," said Jim, "rest a bit, then I guess we had better find a way to get down onto the canal."

Frank answered dully, "Not for me. I've come as far as I can."

"Don't talk that way."

"I'm telling you, Jim, that's how it is."

Jim puzzled at it. "I tell you what—I'll search around. These places are always honeycombed underneath. I'll find a place for us to hole up over night."

"Just as you like."

"You just stay here." He started to leave, then suddenly became aware that Willis was not with him. He then recalled that the bouncer had jumped down when they entered the city. "Willis—where's Willis?"

"How would I know?"

"I've got to find him. Oh, Willis! Hey, Willis! Come, boy!" His voice echoed around the dead square.

"Hi, Jim!"

It was Willis, rightly enough, his voice reaching Jim from some distance. Presently he came into sight. But he was not alone; he was being carried by a Martian.

The Martian came near them, dropped his third leg, and leaned down. His voice boomed gently at Jim. "What's he saying, Frank?"

"Huh? Oh, I don't know. Tell him to go away."

The Martian spoke again. Jim abandoned the attempt to use Frank as a translator and concentrated on trying to understand. He spotted the question symbol, in the inverted position; the remark was an invitation or a suggestion of some sort. Following it was the operator of motion coupled with some radical that meant nothing to Jim.

He answered it with the question symbol alone, hoping that the native would repeat himself. Willis answered instead. "Come along, Jim boy—fine place!"

Why not? he said to himself and answered, "Okay, Willis." To the Martian he replied with the symbol of great assent, racking his throat to produce the unEarthly triple guttural required. The Martian repeated it, inverted, then picked up the leg closest to them and walked rapidly away without turning around. He had gone about twenty-five yards when he seemed to notice that he was not being followed. He backed up just as rapidly and used the general inquiry symbol in the sense of "What's wrong?"

"Willis," Jim said urgently, "I want him to carry Frank."

"Carry Frank boy?"

"Yes, the way Gekko carried him."

"Gekko not here. This K'boomch."

"His name is K'boomk?"

"Sure—K'boomch," Willis agreed, correcting Jim's pronunciation.

"Well, I want K'boomch to carry Frank like Gekko carried him."

Willis and the Martian mooed and croaked at each other for a moment, then Willis said, "K'boomch wants to know does Jim boy know Gekko."

"Tell him we are friends, water friends."

"Willis already tell him."

"How about Frank?" But it appeared that Willis had already told his new acquaintance about that, too, for K'boomch enclosed Frank in two palm flaps and lifted him up. Frank opened his eyes, then closed them. He seemed indifferent to what happened to him.

Jim trotted after the Martian, stopping only to grab up Frank's skates from where he had abandoned them on the metal slab. The Martian led him into a huge building that seemed even larger inside than out, so richly illuminated in glowing lights were the walls. The Martian did not tarry but went directly into an archway in the far wall; it was a ramp tunnel entrance, leading down.

The Martians appear never to have invented stair steps, or more likely never needed them. The low surface gravity of Mars, only 38% of that of Earth, permits the use of ramps which would be disastrously steep on Earth. The Martian led Jim down a long sequence of these rapid descents.

Presently Jim discovered, as he had once before under Cynia city, that the air pressure had increased. He raised his mask with a feeling of great relief; he had not had it off for more than twenty-four hours. The change in pressure had come abruptly; he knew from this that it had not resulted from descent alone, nor had they come deep enough to make any great difference in pressure.

Jim wondered how the trick was accomplished. He decided that it had pressure locks beat all hollow.

They left the ramps and entered a large domed chamber, evenly lighted from the ceiling itself. Its walls were a continuous series of archways. K'boomch stopped and spoke again to Jim, another inquiry in which he used the name Gekko.

Jim reached into his memory and carefully phrased a simple declaration: "Gekko and I have shared water. We are friends."

The Martian seemed satisfied; he led the way into one of the side rooms and placed Frank gently on the floor. The door closed behind them, sliding silently into place. It was a smallish room, for Martians, and contained several resting frames. K'boomch arranged his ungainly figure on one of them.

Suddenly Jim felt heavy and sat down rather unexpectedly on the floor. The feeling persisted and with it a slight giddiness; he stayed seated. "Are you all right, Frank?" he asked.

Frank muttered something. His breathing seemed labored

and rough. Jim took off Frank's mask and touched his face; it was hot.

There was nothing that he could do for Frank at the moment. The heavy feeling continued. The Martian did not seem disposed to talk and Jim did not feel up to attempting a conversation in the dominant tongue in any case. Willis had withdrawn into a ball. Jim lay down beside Frank, closed his eyes, and tried not to think.

He felt a moment of lightness, almost of vertigo, then felt heavy again and wondered what he was coming down with. He lay still for a few more minutes, to be disturbed presently by the native bending over him and speaking. He sat up and discovered that he felt fine again. K'boomch scooped up Frank and they left the room.

The great domed chamber outside looked the same, except that it now held a crowd of Martians, thirty or more of them. When K'boomch and his two burdens, followed by Jim, came out the archway one of them separated himself from the group and stepped forward. He was rather short as Martians go. "Jim-Marlowe," he stated, with the vocative symbol.

"Gekko!" yelled Jim, echoed by Willis.

Gekko bent over him. "My friend," he boomed softly in his own tongue. "My little, crippled friend." He raised Jim up and carried him away, the other Martians retreating to make way.

Gekko moved rapidly through a series of tunnels. Jim, looking back, could see that K'boomch and the rest of his party were close behind, so he let matters drift. Gekko turned presently into a medium-sized chamber and put Jim down. Frank was deposited by him. Frank blinked his eyes and said, "Where are we?"

Jim looked around. The room held several resting frames, set in a circle. The ceiling was domed and simulated the sky. On one wall a canal flowed past, in convincing miniature. Elsewhere on the curved wall was the silhouette of a Martian city, feathery towers floating in the air. Jim knew those towers, knew of what city they were the signature; Jim knew this room.

It was the very room in which he had "grown together" with Gekko and his friends.

"Oh, my gosh, Frank—we're back in Cynia."

"Huh?" Frank sat up suddenly, glared around him—then lay back down and shut his eyes tightly.

Jim did not know whether to laugh or to cry. All that effort! All their striving to escape and to get home, Frank's gallant refusal to give up in the face of sickness and body weariness, the night in the desert cabbage—and here they were not three miles from Cynia station.

VIII

THE OTHER WORLD

JIM SET UP housekeeping—or hospital-keeping—in the smallest room that Gekko could find for him. There had been a "growing together" immediately after their arrival. On its conclusion Jim had found, as before, that his command of the dominant tongue was improved. He had made Gekko understand that Frank was sick and needed quiet.

Gekko offered to take over Frank's care, but Jim refused. Martian therapy might cure Frank—or it might kill him. He asked instead for a plentiful supply of drinking water—his right, now that he was a "water friend," almost a tribal brother—and he asked for the colorful Martian silks that had been used by the boys in place of resting frames. From these silks Jim made a soft bed for Frank and a nest nearby for himself and Willis. He bedded Frank down, roused him enough to get him to drink deeply of water, and then waited for his friend to get well.

The room was quite comfortably warm; Jim took off his outdoors suit, stretched, and scratched. On second thought he peeled off Frank's elastic suit as well and covered him with a layer of flame-colored cloth. After that he dug into Frank's travel bag and looked over the food supply. Up to now, he had been too busy and too tired to worry about his stomach; now the very sight of the labels made him drool. He picked out a can of synthetic orange juice, vitamin fortified, and a can of simulated chicken filet. The latter had started life in a yeast tank at North Colony, but Jim was used to yeast proteins and the flavor was every bit as tempting as white breast of chicken. Whistling, he got out his knife and got busy.

Willis had wandered off somewhere but he did not miss him. Subconsciously he was not disposed to worry about Willis while they were both in a native city; the place was filled with an atmosphere of peace and security. In fact Jim hardly thought about his patient until he had finished and wiped his mouth.

Frank was still sleeping but his breathing was noisy and his face still flushed. The air in the room, though warm and of satisfactory pressure, was Mars dry. Jim got a handkerchief from his bag, wet it, and put it over Frank's face. From time to time he moistened it again. Later he got another handkerchief, doused it, and tied it around his own face.

Gekko came in with Willis tagging along. "Jim-Marlowe," he stated and settled himself. "Gekko," Jim answered and went on with moistening Frank's face cloth. The Martian remained so quiet for so long that Jim decided that he must have retreated into his "other world" but, when Jim looked at him, Gekko's eyes showed lively, alert interest.

After a long wait he asked Jim what he was doing and why.

Jim tried to explain that his kind must breathe water as well as air but his Martian vocabulary, despite the "growing together," was not up to the strain it placed on it. He gave up and there was another long silence. Eventually the Martian left, Willis with him.

Presently Jim noticed that the face cloths, both his and Frank's, were not drying out rapidly. Shortly they were hardly drying at all. He took off his, as it made him uncomfortable, and decided that it must be uncomfortable for Frank as well; he stopped using them entirely.

Gekko returned. After only ten minutes of silence he spoke, showing thereby almost frantic haste for his kind. He wanted to know if the water that flies with the air was now sufficient? Jim assured him that it was and thanked him. After twenty minutes or so of silence Gekko again left. Jim decided to go to bed. It had been a long, hard day and the previous night could hardly be called a night of rest. He looked around for some way to switch off the light but could find none. Giving up, he lay down, pulled a polychrome sheet up to his chin, and went to sleep.

"Hey, Jim—wake up."

Blearily Jim opened his eyes, and closed them. "Go away."

"Come on. Snap out of it. I've been awake the past two hours, while you snored. I want to know some things."

"What do you want to know? Say—how do you feel?"

"Me?" said Frank. "I feel fine. Why shouldn't I? Where are we?"

Jim looked him over. Frank's color was certainly better and his voice sounded normal, the hoarseness all gone. "You were plenty sick yesterday," he informed him. "I think you were out of your head."

Frank wrinkled his forehead. "Maybe I was. I've sure had the darnedest dreams. There was a crazy one about a desert cabbage——"

"That was no dream."

"What?"

"I said that was no dream, the desert cabbage—nor any of the rest of it. Do you know where we are?"

"That's what I was asking you."

"We're in Cynia, that's where we are. We——"

"In *Cynia?*"

Jim tried to give Frank a coherent account of the preceding two days. He was somewhat hampered by the item of their sudden translation from far up the canal back to Cynia, because he did not understand it clearly himself. "I figure it's a sort of a subway paralleling the canal. You know —a subway, like you read about."

"Martians don't do that sort of engineering."

"Martians built the canals."

"Yes, but that was a long, long time ago."

"Maybe they built the subway a long time ago. What do you know about it?"

"Well—nothing, I guess. Never mind. I'm hungry. Anything left to eat?"

"Sure." Jim got up and looked around. Willis was still missing.

"I'd like to find Gekko and ask him where Willis is," he fretted.

"Nuts," said Frank. "Let's eat breakfast."

"Well . . . all right."

Once the meal was over, Frank opened the larger question. "Okay, so we are in Cynia. We've still got to get home and fast. The question is: how do we go about it? Now as I see it, if these Martians could bring us back here so fast they can turn around and put us back where they found us and then we can head home up the east leg of Strymon. How does that strike you?"

"It sounds all right, I guess," Jim answered, "but——"

"Then the first thing to do is to find Gekko and try to arrange it, without fiddling around."

"The first thing to do," Jim contradicted, "is to find Willis."

"Why? Hasn't he caused enough trouble? Leave him; he's happy here."

"Frank, you take entirely the wrong attitude toward Willis. Didn't he get us out of a jam? If it hadn't been for Willis, you'd be coughing your lungs out in the desert."

"If it hadn't been for Willis, we wouldn't have been in that jam in the first place."

"Now that's not fair. The truth is——"

"Skip it, skip it. Okay, go find Willis."

Jim left Frank to clean up the litter of breakfast and set out. Although he was never able thereafter to give a fully coherent account of just what happened to him on this errand, certain gross facts are clear. He started by looking for Gekko, asking for him of the first Martian he met in the corridors by the barbarous expedient of voicing the general inquiry followed by Gekko's name.

Jim was not and probably never would be a competent linguist, but his attempt worked. The first Martian he encountered took him to another, as an Earthly citizen might lead a foreigner to a policeman. This Martian took him to Gekko.

Jim had no great trouble in explaining to Gekko that he wanted Willis returned to him. Gekko listened, then explained gently that what Jim wanted was impossible.

Jim started over again, sure that his own poor command of the language had caused misunderstanding. Gekko let him finish, then made it quite clear that he understood correctly what it was that Jim wanted, but that Jim could not have it—could not have Willis. No. Gekko was sorrowful to have to refuse his friend with whom he had shared the pure water of life, but this thing could not be.

Under the direct influence of Gekko's powerful personality Jim understood most of what was said and guessed the rest. Gekko's refusal was unmistakable. It is not important that Jim did not have his gun with him; Gekko could not inspire the hatred in him that Howe did. For one thing Gekko's warm sympathy poured over him in a flood; nevertheless Jim was thunderstruck, indignant, and quite unable to accept the verdict. He stared up at the Martian for a long moment. Then he walked away abruptly, not choosing his direction and shouting for Willis as he did so. "Willis! Oh, Willis! Here, Willis boy—come to Jim!"

The Martian started after him, each stride three of Jim's. Jim ran, still shouting. He turned a corner, came face to face with three natives and darted between their legs and beyond. Gekko got into a traffic jam with them which required timewasting exercise of Martian protocol to straighten out. Jim got considerably ahead.

He stuck his head into every archway he came to and shouted. One such led into a chamber occupied by Martians frozen in that trancelike state they call visiting the "other world." Jim would no more have disturbed a Martian in a trance, ordinarily, than an American western frontier child would have teased a grizzly—but he was in no shape to care or notice; he shouted in there, too, thereby causing an unheard-of and unthinkable disturbance. The least response was violent trembling; one poor creature was so disturbed that he lifted abruptly all of his legs and fell to the floor.

Jim did not notice; he was already gone, shouting into the next chamber.

Gekko caught up with him and scooped him up with two great hand flaps. "Jim-Marlowe!" he said. "Jim-Marlowe, my friend——"

Jim sobbed and beat on the Martian's hard thorax with both his fists. Gekko endured it for a moment, then wrapped a third palm flap around Jim's arms, securing him. Jim looked wildly up at him. "Willis," he said in his own language, "I want Willis. You've got no right!"

Gekko cradled him and answered softly, "I have no power. This is beyond me. We must go to the other world." He moved away. Jim made no answer, tired by his own outburst. Gekko took a ramp downward, then another and another. Down and down he went, much deeper than Jim had ever been before, deeper perhaps than any terrestrial had ever been. On the upper levels they passed other Martians; farther down there were none.

At last Gekko halted in a small chamber far underground. It was exceptional in that it was totally without decoration; its plain, pearl-gray walls seemed almost unMartian. Gekko laid Jim on the floor here and said, "This is a gate to the other world."

Jim picked himself up. "Huh?" he said. "What do you mean?" and then carefully rephrased the question in the dominant tongue. He need not have bothered; Gekko did not hear him.

Jim craned his neck and looked up. Gekko stood utterly motionless, all legs firmly planted. His eyes were open but lifeless. Gekko had crossed over into the "other world."

"For the love of Mike," Jim fretted, "he sure picks a sweet

time to pull a stunt like that." He wondered what he ought to do, try to find his way to the upper levels alone or wait for Gekko. Natives were reputed to be able to hold a trance for weeks at a time, but Doc MacRae had pooh-poohed such stories.

He decided to wait for a while at least and sat down on the floor, hands clasped around his knees. He felt considerably calmed down and in no special hurry, as if Gekko's boundless calm had flowed over into him while the native had carried him.

After a while, an indefinitely long while, the room grew darker. Jim was not disturbed; he was vastly content, feeling again the untroubled happiness that he had known in his two experiences of "growing together."

A tiny light appeared at great distance in the darkness and grew. But it did not illuminate the small pearl-gray room; it built up an outdoor scene instead. It was as if a stereo-movie projector were being used to project New Hollywood's best work, in full, natural color. That it was not an importation from Earth Jim knew, for the scene, while utterly realistic, had no slick commercial finish, no plot.

He seemed to be seeing a grove of canal plants from a viewpoint about a foot off the ground. The viewpoint shifted steadily and erratically as if the camera were being trucked on a very low dolly here and there through the stalks of the canal plants. The viewpoint would shift quickly for a few feet, stop, then change direction and move again, but it never got very far off the ground. Sometimes it would wheel in a full circle, a panorama of three hundred and sixty degrees.

It was during one of these full rotations that he caught sight of a water-seeker.

It would not have been strange if he had not recognized it as such, for it was enormously magnified. As it charged in, it filled the entire screen. But it was impossible not to recognize those curving scimitar claws, the grisly horror of the gaping sucker orifice, those pounding legs—and most particularly the stomach-clutching revulsion the thing inspired. Jim could almost smell it.

The viewpoint from which he saw it did not change; it was frozen to one spot while the foul horror rushed directly at him in the final death charge. At the last possible instant, when the thing filled the screen, something happened. The face—or where the face should have been—disappeared, went to pieces, and the creature collapsed in a blasted ruin.

The picture was wiped out completely for a few moments, replaced by whirling colored turmoil. Then a light, sweet voice said, "Well, aren't you the cute little fellow!" The picture built up again as if a curtain had been lifted and Jim stared at another face almost as grotesque as the faceless horror it replaced.

Although this face occupied the whole screen and was weirdly distorted, Jim had no trouble in placing it as a colonial's respirator mask. What startled him almost out of the personal unawareness with which he was accepting this shadow show was that he recognized the mask. It was decorated with the very tiger stripes that Smythe had painted out for a quarter credit; it was his own, as it used to be.

He heard his own voice say, "You're too little to be wandering around by yourself; another one of those vermin might really get you. I think I'll take you home."

The scene went swinging through the canal growth at a greater height, bobbling up and down to the boy's steps. Presently the point of view came out into open country and showed in the distance the star-shaped lay-out and bubble domes of South Colony.

Jim adjusted to the idea of watching himself, hearing himself, and accepted the notion of seeing things from Willis's viewpoint. The record was quite unedited; it pushed forward in a straight line, complete recollection of everything Willis had seen and heard from the time Jim had first taken him under his protection. Willis's visual recollections were not entirely accurate; they seemed to be affected by his understanding of what he saw and how used to it he was. Jim—the "Jim" in the shadow show—at first seemed to have three legs; it was some time before the imaginary excrescence vanished. Other actors, Jim's mother, old Doc Mac-

Rae, Frank, developed from formless shapes to full though somewhat distorted representations.

On the other hand, every sound was heard with great clarity and complete accuracy. As Jim listened and watched he found that he was savoring sounds of every sort and most especially voices with a new and rich delight.

Most especially he enjoyed seeing himself as Willis saw him. With affection and warm humor he saw himself stripped of dignity but clothed in a lively regard; he was loved but not respected. He, Jim himself, was a great bumbling servant, helpful but maddeningly unreliable in his attentions, like a poorly trained dog. As for other human beings, they were curious creatures, harmless on the whole, but unpredictable traffic hazards. This bouncer-eye view of people amused Jim mightily.

Day by day and week by week the account unfolded, even to the periods of dark and quiet when Willis chose to sleep or was shut up. It carried on to Syrtis Minor and into a bad time when Jim was missing. Howe appeared as a despised voice and a pair of legs; Beecher was a faceless nonentity. It continued, step by step, and somehow Jim was neither tired nor bored. He was simply in the continuity and could no more escape from it than could Willis—nor did it occur to him to try. At last it wound up in the Martian city of Cynia and ended in a period of dark and quiet.

Jim stretched his cramped legs; the light was returning. He looked about but Gekko was still deep in his trance. He looked back and found that a door had opened in what had appeared to be blank wall. He looked through and into a room beyond, decorated as Martian rooms so frequently are in careful imitation of an outdoor scene—lush countryside more like the sea bottoms south of Cynia than like the desert.

A Martian was in the room. Jim was never able afterwards to visualize him completely for his face and particularly his eyes compelled attention. An Earthling has no good way to estimate the age of a Martian, yet Jim had the unmistakable impression that this Martian was very old—older than his father, older even than Doc MacRae.

"Jim Marlowe," the native said in clear tones. "Welcome,

Jim Marlowe, friend of my people and friend of mine. I give you water." He spoke in Basic English, in an accent vaguely familiar.

Jim had never heard a Martian speak an Earthly tongue before, but he knew that some of them did speak Basic. It was a relief to be able to answer in his own speech. "I drink with you. May you ever enjoy pure and plentiful water."

"I thank you, Jim Marlowe." No actual water was used and none was needed. There followed a polite period of quiet, during which Jim thought about the Martian's accent. It was oddly familiar; it put him in mind of his father's voice, again it sounded like Doc MacRae.

"You are troubled, Jim Marlowe. Your unhappiness is ours. How may I help you?"

"I don't want anything," Jim answered, "except to go home and take Willis with me. They took Willis away. They shouldn't have done that."

The silence that followed was even longer than before. At last the Martian answered, "When one stands on the ground, one may not see over the horizon—yet Phobos sees all horizons." He hesitated a moment before the word "Phobos." As if in afterthought he added, "Jim Marlowe, I have but lately learned your tongue. Forgive me if I stumble."

"Oh, you speak it beautifully!" Jim said quite sincerely.

"The words I know; the pictures are not clear. Tell me, Jim Marlowe, what is the london-zoo?"

Jim had to ask him to repeat it before it was clear that the Martian asked about the London Zoo. Jim tried to explain, but broke off before he had finished elaborating the idea. The Martian radiated such cold, implacable anger that Jim was frightened.

After a time the Martian's mood changed abruptly and Jim was again bathed in a warm glow of friendliness that poured out of his host like rays from the Sun and was as real as sunshine to Jim. "Jim Marlowe, twice you have saved the little one whom you call 'Willis' from—" He used first a Martian term not known to Jim, then changed it to "water-seekers." "Have you killed many such?"

"Uh, quite a few, I guess," Jim answered, then added, "I kill 'em whenever I see 'em. They're getting too smart to hang around the colonies much."

The Martian appeared to be thinking this over, but when he got around to answering he had again changed the subject. "Jim Marlowe, twice, perhaps three times, you have saved the little one; once, perhaps twice, our little one has saved you. Each time you have grown closer together. Day by day you have grown together until neither one of you is complete without the other. Do not leave here, Jim Marlowe. Stay. You are welcome in my house, a son and a friend."

Jim shook his head. "I have to go home. In fact I have to go home right away. It's a mighty kind offer and I want to thank you but—" He explained as clearly as he could the threat to the welfare of the colony and the urgent need for him to carry the message. "If you please, sir, we—my friend and I—would like to be taken back where K'boomch found us. Only I want Willis back before we go."

"You wish to go back to the city where you were found? You do not wish to go home?"

Jim explained that Frank and he would go home from there. "Now, sir, why don't you ask Willis whether or not he wants to stay or to go home with me?"

The old Martian sighed exactly as Jim's father had been known to sigh after a fruitless family discussion. "There is a law of life and a law of death and both are the law of change. Even the hardest rock is worn away by the wind. You understand, my son and friend, that even if the one you call Willis returns with you, there will come a time when the little one *must* leave you?"

"Uh, yes, I guess so. You mean Willis can come home with me?"

"We will speak to the one you call Willis."

The old one spoke to Gekko, who stirred and muttered in his sleep. Then the three of them wound back up the ramps, with Gekko carrying Jim and the old one following a little behind.

They stopped in a chamber about half way up to the surface. The room was dark when they reached it but it became illuminated as soon as the party entered. Jim saw that the place was lined, floor to ceiling, with little niches and each niche contained a bouncer, as similar, each to the other, as identical twins.

The little fellows raised their eye stalks when the light came on and peered interestedly around. From somewhere in the room came a shout of "Hi, Jim boy!"

Jim looked around but could not pick out the bouncer that had spoken. Before he could do anything about it the phrase had echoed around the room, "Hi, Jim boy! Hi, Jim boy! Hi Jim boy!" each time in Jim's own voice, as borrowed by Willis.

Jim turned back to Gekko in bewilderment. "Which one is Willis?" he demanded, forgetting to speak in the dominant tongue.

The chorus started up again, "Which one is Willis? Which one is Willis? Which— Which— Which one is Willis?"

Jim stepped out into the middle of the room. "Willis!" he commanded, "come to Jim."

Off to his right a bouncer popped out from a middle tier, landed on the floor, and waddled up to him. "Pick up Willis," it demanded. Gratefully, Jim did so.

"Where Jim boy been?" Willis wanted to know.

Jim scratched the bouncer. "You wouldn't understand if I told you. Look, Willis—Jim is about to go home. Does Willis want to go home with him?"

"Jim go?" Willis said doubtfully, as if the unrelenting echoing chorus had made it hard for him to understand.

"Jim go home, right away. Is Willis coming or is Willis going to stay here?"

"Jim go; Willis go," the bouncer announced, stating it as a law of nature.

"Okay, tell Gekko that."

"Why?" Willis asked suspiciously.

"Tell Gekko that, or you'll get left behind. Go on, tell him."

"Okay." Willis addressed Gekko in a series of clucks and croaks. Neither the old Martian nor Gekko made any comment; Gekko picked up the two smaller creatures and the procession continued on up toward the surface. Gekko put them down outside the room assigned to Frank and Jim. Jim carried Willis inside.

Frank looked up as they came in. He was sprawled on the silks and, arranged beside him on the floor, was a meal, as yet untouched. "Well, I see you found him," he commented. "It sure took you long enough."

Jim was suddenly overcome with remorse. He had been gone goodness knows how long. Days? Weeks? That moving-picture thing had covered months, in detail. "Gee, Frank, I'm sorry," he apologized. "Were you worried about me?"

"Worried? What for? I just didn't know whether or not to wait lunch on you. You must have been gone at least three hours."

Three hours? Jim started to object that it had been more like three weeks, then thought better of it. He recalled that he had not eaten while away, nor did he feel anything more than normally hungry.

"Uh— Yeah, sure. Sorry. Look, do you mind waiting lunch a bit longer?"

"Why? I'm starved."

"Because we're leaving, that's why. Gekko and another native are waiting to take us back to that town where K'-boomch found us."

"Well— Okay!" Frank stuffed his mouth full and started to pull on his outdoors suit.

Jim imitated him, both as to eating and dressing. "We can finish lunch in the subway dingus," he said, mumbling with his mouth full. "Don't forget to fill your mask reservoir."

"Don't worry. I won't pull that stunt twice." Frank filled his tank and Jim's, took a big drink of water, and offered the rest to Jim. Moments later they slung their skates over their shoulders and were ready to leave. The party filed through ramps and corridors to the "subway station" hall and stopped at one of the archways.

The old Martian went inside, but, somewhat to Jim's surprise, Gekko bade them good-by. They parted with ritualistic exchange of courtesies appropriate to water friends, then Frank and Jim, with Willis, went inside and the door closed behind them.

The car started up at once. Frank said, "Wups! what is this?" and sat down suddenly. The old Martian, secure on the resting frame, said nothing. Jim laughed.

"Don't you remember the last ride?"

"Not very well. Say, I feel heavy."

"So do I. That's part of the ride. Now how about a bite to eat? It may be a long time before we get another decent meal."

Frank got out the remainder of their lunch. When they had finished Frank thought about it and opened another can. Before they had had a chance to eat its contents—cold baked beans and surrogate pork—his stomach suddenly did a flip-flop. "Hey!" he yelped. "What's happened?"

"Nothing. It was like that last time."

"I thought we had plowed into something."

"No, it's all right, I tell you. Hand me over some of those beans." They ate the beans and waited; after a time the feeling of extra weight left them and Jim knew that they had arrived.

The door of the car compartment opened and they stepped out into a circular hall exactly like the one they had left. Frank looked around in disappointment. "Say, Jim—we haven't gone any place. There's some mistake."

"No, there's not." He turned, intending to speak to the old Martian, but the archway door behind them was already closed. "Oh, that's too bad," he said.

"What's too bad? That they gave us a run-around?"

"They didn't give us a run-around; it's just that this room looks like the one back in Cynia. You'll see when we get up to the surface. No, I was saying 'too bad' because I let—" Jim hesitated, realizing that he had never gotten the old Martian's name. "—because I let the old fellow, not Gekko, the other one, get away without saying good-by."

"Who?"

"You know, the other one. The one that rode with us."

"What do you mean, the other one? I didn't see anybody

but Gekko. And nobody rode with us; we were in there by ourselves."

"Huh? You must be blind."

"You must be nuts."

"Frank Sutton, do you mean to stand there and tell me you didn't see the Martian that rode with us?"

"You heard me the first time."

Jim took a deep breath. "Well, all I've got to say is: if you hadn't had your face buried in your food the whole time and had looked around you occasionally, you'd see more. How in——"

"Forget it, forget it," Frank interrupted, "before you get me sore. There were six Martians, if you like it that way. Let's get on up and outside and see what the score is. We're wasting time."

"Well, all right." They started up the ramps. Jim was very silent; the incident bothered him more than it did Frank.

Part way up they were forced to adjust their masks. Ten minutes or so thereafter they reached a room into which the sunlight came flooding; they hurried through it and outdoors.

A moment later it was Frank's turn to be puzzled and uncertain. "Jim, I know I was light-headed at the time but wasn't, uh—wasn't that town we started from just a one-tower burg?"

"It was."

"This one isn't."

"No, it isn't."

"We're lost."

"That's right."

IX

POLITICS

THEY WERE in a large enclosed courtyard, such as characterizes many Martian buildings. They could make out the tops of the towers of the city, or some of them, but their view was much restricted.

"What do you think we ought to do?" asked Frank.

"Mmm . . . try to find a native and see if we can find out where we've landed. I wish I hadn't let the old fellow get away from us," Jim added. "He spoke Basic."

"You still harping on that?" said Frank. "Anyway I don't think our chances are good; this place looks utterly deserted. You know what I think? I think they've just dumped us."

" 'I think they've just dumped us,' " agreed Willis.

"Shut up. They wouldn't do that," Jim went on to Frank in worried tones. He moved around and stared over the roof of the building. "Say, Frank——"

"Yes?"

"You see those three little towers, just alike? You can just make out their tips."

"Well? What about them?"

"I think I've seen them before."

"Say, I think I have, too!"

They began to run. Five minutes later they were standing on the city wall and there was no longer any doubt about it; they were in the deserted part of Charax. Below them and about three miles away were the bubble domes of South Colony.

Forty minutes of brisk walking, varied with dog-trotting, got them home.

They split up and went directly to their respective homes. "See you later!" Jim called to Frank and hurried away to his father's house. It seemed to take forever for the pressure lock to let him through. Before the pressure had equalized he could hear his mother, echoed by his sister, inquiring via the announcing speaker as to who was at the door, please?—he decided not to answer but to surprise them.

Then he was inside, facing Phyllis whose face was frozen in amazement—only to throw herself around his neck while shouting, "Mother! Mother! Mother! It's Jim! It's Jim!" and Willis was bouncing around the floor and chorusing. "It's Jim! It's Jim!" and his mother was crowding Phyl aside and hugging him and getting his face wet with her tears and Jim himself wasn't feeling any too steady.

He managed to push them away presently. His mother stood back a little and said, "Just let me look at you, darling. Oh, my poor baby! Are you all right?" She was ready to weep again.

"Sure, I'm all right," Jim protested. "Why shouldn't I be? Say, is Dad home?"

Mrs. Marlowe looked suddenly apprehensive. "No, Jim, he's at work."

"I've got to see him right away. Say, Mom, what are you looking funny about?"

"Why, because— Uh, nothing. I'll call your father right away." She went to the phone and called the ecological laboratory. He could hear her guarded tones: "Mr. Marlowe? Dear, this is Jane. Could you come home right away?" and his father's reply, "It wouldn't be convenient. What's up? You sound strange."

His mother glanced over her shoulder at Jim. "Are you alone? Can I be overheard?" His father answered, "What's the matter? Tell me." His mother replied, almost in a whisper, "He's home."

There was a short silence. His father answered, "I'll be there right away."

In the meantime Phyllis was grilling Jim. "Say, Jimmy, what in the world have you been doing?"

Jim started to answer, thought better of it. "Kid, you wouldn't believe me if I told you."

"I don't doubt it. But what *have* you been doing? You've sure got folks in a stew."

"Never mind. Say, what day is it?"

"Saturday."

"Saturday the what?"

"Saturday the fourteenth of Ceres, of course."

Jim was startled. Four days? Only four days since he had left Syrtis Minor? Then as he reviewed it in his mind, he accepted it. Granting Frank's assertion that the time he had spent down under Cynia was only three hours or so, the rest added up. "Gee! I guess I'm in time then."

"What do you mean, 'in time'?"

"Huh? Oh, you wouldn't understand it. Wait a few years."

"Smarty!"

Mrs. Marlowe came away from the phone. "Your father will be right home, Jim."

"So I heard. Good."

She looked at him. "Are you hungry? Is there anything you would like?"

"Sure, fatted calf and champagne. I'm not really hungry, but I could stand something. How about some cocoa? I've been living on cold stuff out of cans for days."

"Cocoa there shall be."

"Better eat what you can now," put in Phyllis. "Maybe you won't get what you want to eat when——"

"Phyllis!"

"But, Mother, I was just going to say that——"

"Phyllis—keep quiet or leave the room."

Jim's sister subsided with muttering. Shortly the cocoa was ready and while Jim was drinking it his father came in. His father shook hands with him soberly as if he were a grown man. "It's good to see you home, Son."

"It feels might good to be home, Dad." Jim gulped the rest of the cocoa. "But look, Dad, I've got a lot to tell you and there isn't any time to waste. Where's Willis?" He looked around. "Anybody see where he went?"

"Never mind Willis. I want to know——"

"But Willis is essential to this, Dad. Oh, Willis! Come here!" Willis came waddling out of the passageway; Jim picked him up.

"All right; you've got Willis," Mr. Marlowe said. "Now pay attention. What is this mess you are in, Son?"

Jim frowned. "It's a little hard to know where to start."

"There's a warrant out for you and Frank!" blurted out Phyllis.

Mr. Marlowe said, "Jane, will you please try to keep your daughter quiet?"

"Phyllis, you heard what I said before!"

"Aw, Mother, everybody knows it!"

"Possibly Jim did not know it."

Jim said, "Oh, I guess I did. They had cops chasing us all the way home."

"Frank came with you?" asked his father.

"Oh, sure! But we gave 'em the slip. Those Company cops are stupid."

Mr. Marlowe frowned. "See here, Jim—I'm going to call up the Resident and tell him you are here. But I'm not going to let you surrender until something a lot more definite is shown to me than I have seen so far, and certainly not until we've had your side of the matter. When you do surrender, Dad will go along with you and stick by you."

Jim sat up straight. "Surrender? What are you talking about, Dad?"

His father suddenly looked very old and tired. "Marlowes don't run away from the law, Son. You know I'll stick by you no matter what you've done. But you've got to face up to it."

Jim looked at his father defiantly. "Dad, if you think Frank and I have beaten our way across better than two thousand miles of Mars just to give up when we get here —well, you've just got another think coming. And anybody that tries to arrest me is going to find it a hard job." Phyllis was listening round-eyed; his mother was quietly dripping tears.

His father said, "Son, you can't take that attitude."

Jim said, "Can't I? Well, I do. Why don't you find out what the score is before you talk about giving me up?" His voice was a bit shrill.

His father bit his lip. His mother said, "Please, James—why don't you wait and hear what he has to say?"

"Of course I want to hear what he has to say," Mr. Marlowe answered irritably. "Didn't I say that? But I can't let my own son sit there and declare himself an outlaw."

"Please, James!"

"Speak your piece, Son."

Jim looked around. "I don't know as I'm so anxious to, now," he said bitterly. "This is a fine homecoming. You'd think I was a criminal or something."

"I'm sorry, Jim," his father said slowly. "Let's keep first things first. Tell us what happened."

"Well . . . all right. But wait a minute—Phyllis said there was a warrant out for me. For what?"

"Well . . . truancy—but that's not important. Actions to the prejudice of good order and discipline at the school and I myself don't know what they mean by that. It doesn't worry me. But the real charges are burglary and theft—and another one they tacked on a day later, escaping arrest."

"Escaping arrest? That's silly! They never caught us."

"So? How about the others?"

"Theft is silly, too. I didn't steal anything from *him*—Howe, I mean, Headmaster Howe—he stole Willis from *me*. And then he laughed at me when I tried to get him back! I'll 'theft' him!"

"Go on with your story."

"The burglary business has got something to it. I busted into his office, or tried to. But he can't prove anything. I'd like to see him show how I could crawl through a ten-inch round hole. And we didn't leave any finger prints." He added. "Anyhow, I had a right to. He had Willis locked up inside. Say, Dad, can't we swear out a warrant against Howe for stealing Willis? Why should he have it all his own way?"

"Wait a minute, now. You've got me confused. If you have a cause for action against the headmaster, I'll certainly back you up in it. But I want to get things straight. What hole? Did you cut a hole in the headmaster's door?"

"No, Willis did."

"Willis! How can he cut anything?"

"Darned if I know. He just grew an arm with a sort of a claw on the end and cut his way out. I called to him and out he came."

Mr. Marlowe rubbed his forehead. "This gets more confusing all the time. How did you boys get here?"

"By subway. You see——"

"By subway!"

Jim looked thwarted. His mother put in, "James dear, I think perhaps he could tell his story better if we just let him tell it straight through, without interrupting."

"I think you are right," Mr. Marlowe agreed. "I'll reserve my questions. Phyllis, get me a pad and pencil."

Thus facilitated, Jim started over and told a reasonably consecutive and complete story, from Howe's announcement of military-school inspections to their translation via Martian "subway" from Cynia to Charax. When Jim had done, Mr. Marlowe pulled his chin. "Jim, if you didn't have a lifetime reputation for stubborn honesty, I'd think you were romancing. As it is, I have to believe it, but it is the most fantastic thing I ever heard."

"You still think I ought to surrender?"

"Eh? No, no—this puts it in a different light. You leave it up to Dad. I'll call the Resident and——"

"Just a second, Dad."

"Eh?"

"I didn't tell you all of it."

"What? You must, Son, if I am to——"

"I didn't want to get my story fouled up with another issue entirely. I'll tell you, but I want to know something. Isn't the colony supposed to be on its way by now?"

"It was supposed to have been," agreed his father. "Migration would have started yesterday by the original schedule. But there has been a two weeks' postponement."

"That's not a postponement, Dad; that's a frame up. The

Company isn't going to allow the colony to migrate this year. They mean to make us stay here all through the winter."

"What? Why, that's ridiculous, Son; a polar winter is no place for terrestrials. But you are mistaken, it's just a post-ponement; the Company is revamping the power system at North Colony and is taking advantage of an unusually late winter to finish it before we get there."

"I'm telling you, Dad, that's just a stall. The plan is to keep the colony here until it's too late and force you to stay here through the winter. I can prove it."

"How?"

"Where's Willis?" The bouncer had wandered off again, checking up on his domain.

"Never mind Willis. You've made an unbelievable charge. What makes you think such a thing? Speak up, Son."

"But I've got to have Willis to prove it. Here, boy! Come to Jim." Jim gave a rapid summary of what he had learned through Willis's phonographic hearing, following which he tried to get Willis to perform.

Willis was glad to perform. He ran over almost all of the boys' conversation of the past few days, repeated a great amount of Martian speech that was incomprehensible out of context, and sang *¿Quién es la Señorita?* But he could not, or would not, recall Beecher's conversation.

Jim was still coaxing him when the phone sounded. Mr. Marlowe said, "Phyllis, answer that."

She trotted back in a moment. "It's for you, Daddy."

Jim shut Willis up; they could hear both ends of the conversation. "Marlowe? This is the Resident Agent. I hear that boy of yours has turned up."

Jim's father glanced over his shoulder, hesitated. "Yes. He's here."

"Well, keep him there. I'm sending a man over to pick him up."

Mr. Marlowe hesitated again. "That's not necessary, Mr. Kruger. I'm not through talking with him. He won't go away."

"Come, come, Marlowe—you can't interfere with orderly legal processes. I'm executing that warrant at once."

"You are? You just think you are." Mr. Marlowe started to

add something, thought better of it, and switched off. The phone sounded again almost at once. "If that's the Resident," he said, "I won't speak to him. If I do, I'll say something I'll regret."

But it was not; it was Frank's father. "Marlowe? Jamie, this is Pat Sutton." The conversation showed that each father had gotten about to the same point with his son.

"We were just about to try to get something out of Jim's bouncer," Mr. Marlowe added. "It seems he overheard a pretty damning conversation."

"Yes, I know," agreed Mr. Sutton. "I want to hear it, too. Hold it till we get there."

"Fine. Oh, by the way—friend Kruger is out to arrest the kids right away. Watch out."

"How well I know it; he just called me. And I put a flea in his ear. 'Bye now!"

Mr. Marlowe switched off, then went to the front door and locked it. He did the same to the door to the tunnels. He was none too soon; the signal showing that someone had entered the pressure lock came on shortly. "Who is it?" called out Jim's father.

"Company business!"

"What sort of Company business and who is it?"

"This is the Resident proctor. I've come for James Marlowe, Junior."

"You might as well go away again. You won't get him." There was a whispered exchange outside the door, then the lock was rattled.

"Open up that door," came another voice. "We have a warrant."

"Go away. I'm switching off the speaker." Mr. Marlowe did so.

The pressure lock indicator showed presently that the visitors had left, but shortly it indicated occupancy again. Mr. Marlowe switched the speaker back on. "If you've come back, you might as well leave," he said.

"What sort of a welcome is this, Jamie my boy?" came Mr. Sutton's voice.

"Oh, Pat! Are you alone?"

"Only my boy Francis and that's all."

They were let in. "Did you see anything of proctors?" Mr. Marlowe inquired.

"Yep, I ran into 'em."

"Pop told them that if they touched me he'd make them sorry," Frank said proudly, "and he would, too."

Jim caught his father's eye. Mr. Marlowe looked away. Mr. Sutton went on, "Now what's this about Jim's pet having evidence for us? Let's crank him up and hear him talk."

"We've been trying to," Jim said. "I'll try again. Here, Willis—" Jim took him in his lap. "Now, look, Willis, do you remember Headmaster Howe?"

Willis promptly became a featureless ball.

"That's not the way to do it," objected Frank. "You remember what set him off before. Hey, Willis." Willis extended his eyes. "Listen to me, chum. 'Good afternoon. Good afternoon, Mark,' Frank continued in a fair imitation of the Agent General's rich, affected tones. " 'Sit down, my boy.' "

" 'Always happy to see you,' " Willis continued in exact imitation of Beecher's voice. He went on from there, reciting perfectly the two conversations he had overheard between the headmaster and the Resident Agent General, and including the meaningless interlude between them.

When he had finished and seemed disposed to continue with all that had followed up to the present moment, Jim shut him off.

"Well," said Jim's father, "what do you think of it, Pat?"

"*I* think it's terrible," put in Jim's mother.

Mr. Sutton screwed up his face. "Tomorrow I am taking myself down to Syrtis Minor and there I shall take the place apart with my two hands."

"An admirable sentiment," agreed Mr. Marlowe, "but this is a matter for the whole colony. I think our first step should be to call a town meeting and let everyone know what we are up against."

"Humph! No doubt you are right but you'll be taking all the fun out of it."

Mr. Marlowe smiled. "I imagine there will be excitement enough to suit you before this is over. Kruger isn't going to like it—and neither is the Honorable Mr. Gaines Beecher."

Mr. Sutton wanted Dr. MacRae to examine Frank's throat and Jim's father decided, over Jim's protest, that it would be a good idea to have him examine Jim as well. The two men escorted the boys to the Doctor's house. There Mr. Marlowe instructed them, "Stay here until we get back, kids. I don't want Kruger's proctors picking you up."

"I'd like to see them try!"

"Me, too."

"I don't want them to try; I want to settle the matter first. We're going over to the Resident's office and offer to pay for the food you kids appropriated and, Jim, I'll offer to pay for the damage Willis did to Headmaster Howe's precious door. Then——"

"But, Dad, we oughtn't to pay for that. Howe shouldn't have locked him up."

"I agree with the kid," said Mr. Sutton. "The food, now, that's another matter. The boys took it; we pay for it."

"You're both right," agreed Mr. Marlowe, "but it's worth it to knock the props out of these ridiculous charges. Then I'm going to swear out a warrant against Howe for attempting to steal, or ēnslave, Willis. What would you say it was, Pat? Steal, or enslave?"

"Call it 'steal'; you'll not be raising side issues, then."

"All right. Then I shall insist that he consult the planet office before taking any action. I think that will stop his clock for the time being."

"Dad," put in Jim, "you aren't going to tell the Resident that we've found out about the migration frame-up, are you? He would just turn around and call Beecher."

"Not just yet, though he's bound to know at the town meeting. He won't be able to call Beecher, then: Deimos sets in two hours." Mr. Marlowe glanced at his watch. "See you later, boys. We've got things to do."

Doctor MacRae looked up as they came in. "Maggie, bar the door!" he called out. "We've got two dangerous criminals."

"Howdy, Doc."

"Come in and rest yourselves. Tell me all about it."

It was fully an hour later that MacRae said, "Well, Frank, I suppose I had better look you over. Then I'll have a look at you, Jim."

"There's nothing wrong with me, Doc."

"Start some more coffee while I take care of Frank." The room was well stocked with the latest diagnostic equipment, but MacRae did not bother with it. He tilted Frank's head back, told him to say *aaaah!*, thumped his chest, and listened to his heart. "You'll live," he decided. "Any kid who can hitch-hike from Syrtis to Charax will live a long time."

" 'Hitch-hike'?" asked Frank.

"Beat your way. It's an expression that was used way back when. Your turn, Jim." He took even less time to dispose of Jim. Then the three friends settled back to visit.

"I want to know more about this night you spent in the cabbage head," Doc announced. "Willis I can understand, since any Martian creature can tuck his tail in and live indefinitely without air. But by rights you two should have smothered. The plant closed up entirely?"

"Oh, yes," Jim assured him, then related the event in more detail. When he got to the point about the flashlight MacRae stopped him.

"That's it, that's it. You didn't mention that before. The flashlight saved your lives, son."

"Huh? How?"

"Photosynthesis. You shine light on green leaf and it can no more help taking in carbon dioxide and giving off oxygen than you can help breathing." The doctor stared at the ceiling, his lips moving while he figured. "Must have been pretty stuffy, just the same; you were short on green leaf surface. What kind of a torch was it?"

"A G.E. 'Midnight Sun.' It *was* stuffy, terribly."

"A 'Midnight Sun' has enough candle power to do the trick. Hereafter I'll carry one if I'm going further than twenty feet from my front stoop. It's a good dodge."

"Something that still puzzles me," said Jim, "is how I could see a movie that covered every bit of the time I've had Willis, minute by minute, without missing anything, and have it turn out to be only three or four hours."

131

"That," Doc said slowly, "is not nearly so mysterious as the other matter, the matter of *why* you were shown this."

"Huh?"

"I've wondered about that, too," put in Frank. "After all, Willis is a pretty insignificant creature—take it easy, Jim! What was the point in running over his biography for Jim? What do you think, Doc?"

"The only hypothesis I've got on that point is so wildly fantastic that I'll keep it to myself, thank you. But on the point of time, Jim—can you think of any way to photograph a person's memories?"

"Uh, no."

"I'll go further and state flatly that it is impossible. Yet you described *seeing* what Willis *remembered*. That suggest anything to you?"

"No," admitted Jim, "it's got me stumped. But I *did* see it."

"Sure, you did—because seeing takes place in the brain and not in the eye. I can close my eyes and 'see' the Great Pyramid shimmering in the desert heat. I can see the donkeys and hear the porters yelling at the tourists. See 'em? Shucks, I can smell 'em—but it's just memory. Now back to what I was saying, Jim. When only one hypothesis covers the facts, you've got to accept it. You saw what the old Martian wanted you to see. Call it hypnosis."

"But— But—" Jim was wildly indignant; it felt like an attack on his very inner being. "But I *did* see it, I tell you. I was there."

"I'll string along with Doc," Frank told him. "You were still seeing things on the trip back."

"The old boy did so make the trip back with us; if you had kept your eyes open, you would have seen him."

"Easy there," cautioned Doc, "if you lugs want to fight, go outside. Has it occurred to you that both of you might be right?"

"What? How could we be?" objected Frank.

"I don't like to put words to it, but I can tell you this: I've lived long enough to know that man does not live by bread alone and that the cadaver I perform an autopsy on is not the man himself. The most wildly impossible philosophy of all is materialism. We'll leave it at that."

Frank was about to object again when the lock signalled visitors; the boys' parents were back. "Come in, come in, gentlemen," the doctor roared. "You're just in time. We were having a go at solipsism. Pull up a pulpit and take part. Coffee?"

"Solipsism, is it?" said Mr. Sutton. "Francis, pay no mind to the old heathen. You listen to what Father Cleary tells you."

"He'll pay no mind to me anyhow," MacRae answered. "That's the healthy thing about kids. How did you make out with the Lord High Executioner?"

Mr. Marlowe chuckled. "Kruger was fit to be tied."

The called meeting of the colonists took place that evening in the town hall, central building of the star-shaped group. Mr. Marlowe and Mr. Sutton, having sponsored the meeting, arrived early. They found the meeting-room doors closed and Kruger's two proctors posted outside. Mr. Marlowe ignored the fact that they had been attempting to arrest Frank and Jim only a few hours ago; he offered them a civil good evening and said, "Let's get the place opened up. People will be arriving any minute now."

The proctors did not move. The senior of them, a man named Dumont, announced, "There'll be no meeting tonight."

"What? Why not?"

"Mr. Kruger's orders."

"Did he say why?"

"No."

"This meeting," Mr. Marlowe told him, "has been properly called and will be held. Stand aside."

"Now, Mr. Marlowe, don't make things tough for yourself. I've got my orders and——"

Mr. Sutton crowded forward. "Let me handle him, Jamie." He hitched at his belt. Behind the men, Frank glanced at Jim with a grin and hitched at *his* belt. All four of them were armed, as were the proctors; the two fathers had decided not to depend on Kruger's self-restraint while waiting for instructions from Syrtis Minor about the warrant.

Dumont looked nervously at Sutton. The colony had no real police force; these two were clerks in the Company's office and proctors only by Kruger's deputization. "You people have got no call to be running around armed to the teeth, inside the colony," he complained.

"Oh, so that's it?" Mr. Sutton said sweetly. "Well, this job calls for no gun. Here, Francis—hold my heater." With empty holster he advanced on them. "Now would you like to be tossed out gently or would you prefer to bounce?"

For years before coming to Mars Mr. Sutton had used something other than his engineering degree to dominate tough construction gangs. He was not much bigger than Dumont but immeasurably tougher. Dumont backed into his cohort and stepped on his toes. "Now see here, Mr. Sutton, you've no— Hey! Mr. Kruger!"

They all looked around. The Resident was approaching. He took in the scene and said briskly, "What's this? Sutton, are you interfering with my men?"

"Not a bit of it," denied Mr. Sutton. "They were interfering with me. Tell them to stand aside."

Kruger shook his head. "The meeting is canceled.

Mr. Marlowe stepped forward. "By whom?"

"*I* canceled it."

"By what authority? I have the approval of all councilors and will, if necessary, get you the names of twenty colonists." Twenty colonists could call a meeting without permission from the council, under the colony's rules.

"That's beside the point. The rule reads that meetings are to consider matters 'of public interest'; it cannot be construed as 'of public interest' to agitate about criminal indictments in advance of trial—and I won't let you take advantage of the rules to do so. After all, I have the final word. I do not intend to surrender to mob rule and agitation."

A crowd was forming, colonists come to the meeting. Marlowe said, "Are you through?"

"Yes, except to say that these others and you yourself should return to your quarters."

"They will do as they please—and so will I. Mr. Kruger, I am amazed to hear you say that a civil-rights case is not of public interest. Our neighbors here have boys who are still under the care, if you call it that, of Headmaster Howe; they are interested in how their sons are treated. However, that is not the purpose of the meeting. I give you my word that neither Mr. Sutton nor I intend to ask the colony to take any action about the charges against our sons. Will you accept that and withdraw your proctors?"

"What is the purpose, then?"

"It's a matter of urgent interest to every member of he colony. I'll discuss it inside."

"Hummph!"

By this time several councilors were in the crowd. One of them, Mr. Juan Montez, stepped forward. "Just a minute. Mr. Marlowe, when you called me about this meeting, I had no notion that the Resident objected."

"The Resident has no option in the matter."

"Well, that's never come up before. He does have a veto over actions of meetings. Why don't you tell us what the meeting is for?"

"Don't give in, Jamie!" It was Doctor MacRae; he shouldered forward. "What kind of nincompoop are you, Montez? I'm sorry I voted for you. We meet when it suits us, not when Kruger says we may. How about it, folks?"

There was a murmur of approval. Mr. Marlowe said, "I wasn't going to tell him, Doc. I want everybody here and the doors closed when I talk."

Montez went into a huddle with other councilors. Out of it came Hendrix, the chairman. "Mr. Marlowe, just to keep things regular, will you tell the council why you want this meeting?"

Jim's father shook his head. "You okayed the meeting. Otherwise I would have collected twenty signatures and forced a meeting. Can't you stand up to Kruger?"

"We don't need them, Jamie," MacRae assured him. He turned to the crowd, now growing fast. "Who wants a meeting? Who wants to hear what Marlowe has to tell us?"

"I do!" came a shout.

"Who's that? Oh—Kelly. All right, Kelly and I make two. Are there eighteen more here who don't have to ask Kruger for permission to sneeze? Speak up."

There was another shout and another. "That's three—and four." Seconds later MacRae called off the twentieth; he turned to the Resident. "Get your stooges out of that doorway, Kruger."

Kruger sputtered. Hendrix whispered with him, then motioned the two proctors away. They were only too happy to treat this as a relayed order from Kruger; the crowd poured into the hall.

Kruger took a seat in the rear; ordinarily he sat on the platform.

Jim's father found that none of the councilors cared to preside; he stepped to the platform himself. "Let's elect a chairman," he announced.

"You run it, Jamie." It was Doc MacRae.

"Let's have order, please. Do I hear a nomination?"

"Mr. Chairman——"

"Yes, Mr. Konski?"

"I nominate you."

"Very well. Now let's have some others." But there were none; he kept the gavel by unanimous consent.

Mr. Marlowe told them that news had come to him which vitally affected the colony. He then gave the bald facts about how Willis had come into Howe's hands. Kruger stood up. "Marlowe!"

"Address the chair, please."

"Mr. Chairman," Kruger acceded sourly, "you said this meeting was not to stir up sympathy for your son. You are simply trying to keep him from having to take his medicine. You——"

Mr. Marlowe pounded his gavel. "You're out of order. Sit down."

"I won't sit down. You had the bare-faced gall to——"

"Mr. Kelly, I appoint you sergeant-at-arms. Keep order. Pick your own deputies."

Kruger sat down. Mr. Marlowe went on, "This meeting has nothing to do with the charges against my son and Pat Sutton's boy, but the news I have came through them. You've all seen Martian roundheads—bouncers, the kids call them, and you know their amazing ability to repeat sounds. Probably most of you have heard my son's pet perform. It happened that this particular roundhead was within hearing when some things were discussed that we all need to know about. Jim—bring your pet here."

Jim, feeling self-conscious, mounted the platform and sat Willis on the speaker's table. Willis looked around and promptly battened down all hatches. "Jim," his father whispered urgently, "snap him out of it."

"I'll try," agreed Jim. "Come on, boy. Nobody's going to hurt Willis. Come out; Jim wants to talk to you."

His father said to the audience, "These creatures are timid. Please be very quiet." Then, "How about it, Jim?"

"I'm trying."

"Confound it, we should have made a recording."

Willis chose this minute to come out of hiding. "Look, Willis boy," Jim went on, "Jim wants you to talk. Everybody is waiting for Willis to talk. Come on, now. 'Good afternoon. Good afternoon, Mark.'"

Willis picked it up. " 'Sit down, my boy. Always happy to see you.' " He went on, reeling off the words of Howe and Beecher.

Somebody recognized Beecher's voice; there was a muffled exclamation as he passed his knowledge on. Mr. Marlowe made frantic shushing signs.

Presently, as Beecher was expounding by proxy his theory of "legitimate graft," Kruger got up. Kelly placed hands on his shoulders and pushed him down. Kruger started to protest; Kelly placed a hand over Kruger's mouth. He then smiled; it was something he had been wanting to do ever since Kruger had first been assigned to the colony.

The audience got restless between the two significant conversations; Mr. Marlowe promised by pantomime that the best was yet to come. He need not have worried; Willis, once wound up, was as hard to stop as an after-dinner speaker.

There was amazed silence when he had finished, then a

murmur that became a growl. It changed to uproar as everyone tried to talk at once. Marlowe pounded for order and Willis closed up. Presently Andrews, a young technician, got the floor.

"Mr. Chairman . . . we know how important this is, *if* it's true—but how reliable is that beastie?"

"Eh? I don't think it's possible for one of them to repeat other than *verbatim*. Is there a psychological expert present who might give us an opinion? How about you, Dr. Ibañez?"

"I agree, Mr. Marlowe. A roundhead can originate speech on its mental level, but a speech such as we just heard is something it has listened to. It repeats parrot-fashion exactly what it has heard. I doubt if such a 'recording,' if I may call it that, may be modified after it has been impressed on the animal's nervous system; it's an involuntary reflex—complicated and beautiful, but reflex nevertheless."

"Does that satisfy you, Andy?"

"Uh, no. Everybody knows that a bouncer is just a super-parrot and not smart enough to lie. But is that the Resident General's voice? It sounds like it, but I've only heard him over the radio."

Someone called out, "It's Beecher. I had to listen to his drivel often enough, when I was stationed at Syrtis."

Andrews shook his head. "Sure, it sounds like him, but we've got to *know*. It could be a clever actor."

Kruger had been quiet, in a condition resembling shock. The revelation had come as a surprise to him, too, as Beecher had not dared trust anyone on the spot. But Kruger's conscience was not easy; there were tell-tale signs in his own despatch file that Willis's report was correct; migration required a number of routine orders from the planet office. He was uncomfortably aware that none of the proper groundwork had been laid if, as was the official claim, migration were to take place in less than two weeks.

But Andrews' comment gave him a straw to clutch. Standing, he said, "I'm glad somebody has sense enough not to be swindled. How long did it take you to teach him that, Marlowe?"

Kelly said, "Shall I gag him, chief?"

"No. This has to be met. I suppose it's a matter of whether or not you believe my boy and his chum. Do any of you wish to question them?"

A long, lean, lanky individual unfolded himself from a rear seat. "I can settle it."

"Eh? Very well, Mr. Toland, you have the floor."

"Got to get some apparatus. Take a few minutes." Toland was an electronics engineer and sound technician.

"Oh—I think I see what you mean. You'll need a comparison model of Beecher's voice, won't you?"

"Sure. But I've got all I need. Every time Beecher made a speech, Kruger wanted it recorded."

Volunteers were found to help Toland, then Marlowe suggested that it was time for a stretch. At once Mrs. Pottle stood up. "Mr. Marlowe!"

"Yes, Mrs. Pottle. Quiet, everybody."

"I for one will not remain here one minute longer and listen to this nonsense! The idea of making such charges against dear Mr. Beecher! To say nothing of what you let that awful man Kelly do to Mr. Kruger! And as for that beast—" She pointed to Willis. "It is utterly unreliable, as I know full well." She paused to snort, then said, "Come, dear," to Mr. Pottle, and started to flounce out.

"Stop her, Kelly!" Mr. Marlowe went on quietly, "I had hoped that no one would try to leave until we reached a decision. If the colony decides to act it may be to our advantage to keep it as a surprise. Will the meeting authorize me to take steps to see that no scooter leaves the colony until you have made up your minds about the issue?"

There was just one "no," from Mrs. Pottle. "Conscript some help, Mr. Kelly," Marlowe ordered, "and carry out the will of the meeting."

"Right, chief!"

"You can go now, Mrs. Pottle. Not you, Mr. Kruger." Mr. Pottle hesitated in bewilderment, then trotted after his wife.

Toland returned and set up his apparatus on the platform. With Jim's help, Willis was persuaded to perform again, this time into a recorder. Shortly Toland held up his hand. "That's enough. Let me find some matching words." He selected "colony," "company," "afternoon," and "Martian" because they were easy to find in each recording, Willis's and an identified radio speech of the Resident General. Each he checked with care, throwing complex standing waves on the bright screen of an oscilloscope, waves that ear-marked the peculiar timbre of an individual's voice as certainly as a finger print would identify his body.

At last he stood up. "It's Beecher's voice," he said flatly.

Jim's father again had to pound for order. When he had got it, he said, "Very well—what is your pleasure?"

Someone shouted, "Let's lynch Beecher." The chairman suggested that they stick to practical objectives.

Someone else called out, "What's Kruger got to say about it?"

Marlowe turned to Kruger. "Mr. Resident Agent, you speak for the Company. What about it?"

Kruger wet his lips. "If one assumes that that beast is actually reporting statements of the Agent General——"

"Quit stalling!"

"Toland proved it!"

Kruger's eyes darted around; he was faced with a decision impossible for a man of his temperament. "Well, it's really no business of mine," he said angrily. "I'm about to be transferred."

MacRae got up. "Mr. Kruger, you are custodian of our welfare. You mean to say you won't stand up for our rights?"

"Well, now, Doctor, I work for the Company. If this is its policy—and I'm not admitting it—you can't expect me to go against it."

"I work for the Company, too," the Doctor growled, "but I didn't sell myself to it, body and soul." His eyes swept the crowd. "How about it, folks? Shall we throw him out on his ear?"

Marlowe had to bang for order. "Sit down, Doctor. We haven't time to waste on trivia."

"Mr. Chairman——"

"Yes, Mrs. Palmer?"

"What do you think we ought to do?"

"I would rather that suggestions came from the floor."

"Oh, nonsense—you've known about it longer than we have; you must have an opinion. Speak up."

Marlowe saw that her wish was popular. "Very well, I speak for myself and Mr. Sutton. By contract we are entitled to migrate and the Company is obligated to let us. I say go ahead and do so, at once."

"I so move!"

"I second!"

"Question!"—"Question!"

"Is there debate?" asked Marlowe.

"Just a moment, Mr. Chairman—" The speaker was one Humphrey Gibbs, a small precise individual. "—we are acting hastily and, if I may say so, not in proper procedure. We have not exhausted our possible reliefs. We should communicate with Mr. Beecher. It may be that there are good reasons for this change in policy——"

"How are *you* going to like a hundred below!"

"Mr. Chairman, I really must insist on order."

"Let him have his say," Marlowe ordered.

"As I was saying, there may be good reasons, but the Company board back on Earth is perhaps not fully aware of conditions here. If Mr. Beecher is unable to grant us relief, then we should communicate with the board, reason with them. But we should not take the law into our own hands. If worse comes to worst, we have a contract; if forced to do so, we can always sue." He sat down.

MacRae got up again. "Anybody mind if I talk? I don't want to hog the proceedings." Silence gave approval; he went on, "So this panty-waist wants to sue! With the temperature outside a hundred and thirty below by the time he has 'exhausted his means'—and us!—and with the rime frost a foot deep on the ground he wants it put on some judge's calendar, back on Earth, and hire a lawyer!

"If you want a contract enforced, you have to enforce it yourself. You know what lies behind this; it showed up last season when the Company cut down on the household allowance and started charging excess baggage. I warned you then—but the board was a hundred million miles away and you paid rather than fight. The Company hates the expense of moving us, but more important they are very anxious to move more immigrants in here faster than we can take them; they think they see a cheap way out by keeping both North Colony and South Colony filled up all the time, instead of building more buildings. As Sister Gibbs put it, they don't realize the conditions here and they don't know that we can't do effective work in the winter.

"The question is not whether or not we can last out a polar winter; the Eskimo caretakers do that every season. It isn't just a matter of contract; it's a matter of whether we are going to be free men, or are we going to let our decisions be made for us on another planet, by men who have never set foot on Mars!

"Just a minute—let me finish! We are the advance guard. When the atmosphere project is finished, millions of others will follow. Are they going to be ruled by a board of absentee owners on Terra? Is Mars to remain a colony of Earth? Now is the time to settle it!"

There was dead silence, then scattered applause. Marlowe said, "Is there more debate?"

Mr. Sutton got up. "Doc has something there. It was never in my blood to love absentee landlords."

Kelly called out, "Right you are, Pat!"

Jim's father said, "I rule that subject out of order. The question before the house is to migrate, at once, and nothing else. Are you ready for the question?"

They were—and it was carried unanimously. If any refrained from voting, at least they did not vote against. That matter settled, by another ballot they set up an emergency committee, the chairman to hold power subject to review by the committee, and the committee's decisions to be subject to review by the colony.

James Marlowe, Senior, was elected chairman. Dr. MacRae's name was proposed but he refused to let it be considered. Mr. Marlowe got even with him by sticking him on the committee.

South Colony held at the time five hundred and nine

persons, from the youngest baby to old Doc MacRae. There were eleven scooters on hand; enough but barely enough to move everyone at one time, provided they were stacked almost like freight and each person was limited to a few pounds only of hand baggage. A routine migration was usually made in three or more sections, with extra scooters provided from Syrtis Minor.

Jim's father decided to move everyone at once and hoped that events would permit sending back for personal possessions. The squawks were many, but he stood by his guns, the committee ratified and no one tried to call a town meeting. He set dawn Monday as the zero hour.

Kruger was allowed to keep his office; Marlowe preferred to run the show from his own. But Kelly, who remained a sort of *de facto* chief of police, was instructed to keep a constant watch over him. Kelly called Marlowe Sunday afternoon. "Hey, chief, what do you know? A couple of Company cops just arrived by scooter to take your boy and the Sutton kid back to Syrtis."

Marlowe considered it. Kruger must have phoned Beecher the moment he heard that the boys were home, he decided. "Where are they now?"

"Right here, in Kruger's office. *We* arrested *them*."

"Bring them over. I'd like to question them."

"Right."

They showed up shortly, two very disgruntled men, disarmed and escorted by Kelly and an assistant. "That's fine, Mr. Kelly. No, no need to stay—I'm armed."

When Kelly and his deputy had left, one of the Company men said, "You can't get away with this, you know."

"You're not hurt," Marlowe said reasonably, "and you'll get your guns back presently. I just want to ask you some questions." But all he had gotten out of them, several minutes later, was a series of begrudged negative answers. The intra-colony phone sounded again; Kelly's face appeared on the screen. "Chief? You wouldn't believe it——".

"Wouldn't believe what?"

"That old fox Kruger has skipped in the scooter those two birds came in on. I didn't even know he could drive."

Marlowe's calm face concealed his feelings. After a short time he answered, "Departure time is stepped up to sundown, today. Drop everything and get the word around." He consulted a chart. "That's two hours and ten minutes from now."

The squawks were louder even than before; nevertheless as the Sun touched the horizon, the first scooter got underway. The rest followed at thirty second intervals. As the Sun disappeared the last one shoved off and the colony was headed north on its seasonal migration.

X

"WE'RE BOXED IN!"

FOUR OF THE SCOOTERS were older types and slower, less than two hundred miles per hour top speed. They were placed in the van as pace-setters. Around midnight one of them developed engine trouble; the column had to slow down. About 3 A.M. it quit completely; it was necessary to stop and distribute its passengers among the other scooters—a cold and risky business.

MacRae and Marlowe climbed back into the headquarters car, last in the column. The doctor glanced at his watch. "Planning to stop in Hesperidum now, Skipper?" he asked as the scooter started up. They had passed Cynia station without stopping; Hesperidum lay a short distance ahead, with Syrtis Minor some seven hundred miles beyond it.

Marlowe frowned. "I don't want to. If we lay over at Hesperidum, that means waiting until sundown for ice and a full day's loss of time. With Kruger ahead of us that gives Beecher a whole day in which to figure out a way to stop us. If I were sure the ice would hold after sunrise long enough for us to get there—" He stopped and chewed his lip.

Back at South Colony it was early winter and the canal ice would remain hard until spring, but here they were already close to the equator; the canals froze every night and thawed every day under the extreme daily changes in temperature permitted by Mars' thin blanket of air. North of the equator, where they were headed, the spring floods from the melting northern polar cap had already started; ice formed in the flooding canal currents at night, but it was floe ice, riding with the current, and night clouds helped to save the daytime heat.

"Suppose you do go on through, what's your plan, Skipper?" MacRae persisted.

"Go straight to the boat basin, ramp the scooters, and load whatever boats are there. As soon as the ice is rotten enough for the boats to break through it, start them north. I'd like to have a hundred and fifty or so of us out of Syrtis Minor and headed north before Beecher recovers from his surprise. I haven't any real plan except to keep forcing events so that *he* doesn't have time to plan, either. I want to hand him a set of accomplished facts."

MacRae nodded. "Audacity, that's the ticket. Go ahead with it."

"I want to, but I'm afraid of the ice. If a scooter breaks through there'll be people killed—and my fault."

"Your drivers are smart enough to spread out in echelon once the Sun is up. Jamie, I found out a long time ago that you have to take some chances in this life. Otherwise you are just a vegetable, headed for the soup pot." He paused and peered out past the driver. "I see a light ahead that ought to be Hesperidum. Make up your mind, Jamie."

Marlowe did not answer. After a time the light was behind them.

When the Sun came up Marlowe had his driver cut out of column and take the lead. It was near nine when they passed Syrtis Minor scooter station, without stopping. They ploughed on past the space port and turned right into the boat basin that marked the terminus of the main canal from the north. Marlowe's driver drove onto the ramp while still lowering his crawling gear, with no respect for his runners. The lead car crawled along the ramp and parked; the others closed in behind it.

Out of the headquarters car climbed Marlowe, Kelly, and MacRae, followed by Jim, carrying Willis. Other scooter doors opened and people started getting out. "Tell them to get back into their cars, Kelly," Mr. Marlowe snapped. Hearing this, Jim placed himself behind his father and tried to avoid attracting attention.

Marlowe stared angrily at the basin. There was not a boat in it. Across the basin one small launch was drawn up on skids, its engine dismounted. Finally Marlowe turned to MacRae. "Well, Doc, I'm up a tree; how do I get down?"

"You are no worse off than if you had stopped at Hesperidum."

"And no better."

A man came out of one of the row of warehouses ringing the basin and approached them. "What's all this?" he inquired, staring at the parked scooters. "A circus?"

"It's the seasonal migration."

"Wondered when you folks were coming through. Hadn't heard anything about it."

"Where are all the boats?"

"Still spread out here and there, at the Project camps mostly, I suppose. Not my responsibility. Better call the traffic office."

Marlowe frowned again. "At least you can tell me where the temporary quarters are." To take care of the relays of colonists a warehouse was always set aside at each migration and fitted up as a barracks; the one Company hostelry, Hotel Marsopolis, had only twenty beds.

The man looked puzzled. "Now that you mention it, I don't know of any such preparations being made. Looks like the schedule was kind of fouled up, doesn't it?"

Marlowe swore, realizing his question had been foolish. Beecher, of course, had made no preparations for a migration he did not intend to permit. "Is there a phone around here?"

"Inside, in my office—I'm the warehouse storekeeper. Help yourself."

"Thanks," said Marlowe and started off. MacRae followed him.

"What's your plan, son?"

"I'm going to call Beecher."

"Do you think that's wise?"

"Confound it, I've got to get those people out of those cars. There are young babies in there—and women."

"They're safe."

"Look, Doc, Beecher has got to do *something* about it, now that we're here."

MacRae shrugged. "You're the cook."

Marlowe argued his way past several secretaries and finally got Beecher on the screen. The Agent General looked out at him without recognition. "Yes? Speak up, my good man, what is this urgent business?"

"My name is Marlowe. I'm executive chairman of the colonists from South Colony. I want to know——"

"Oh, yes! The famous Mr. Marlowe. We saw your tattered army coming through." Beecher turned away and said something in an aside. Kruger's voice answered him.

"Well, now that we are here, what are you going to do about us?"

"Do? Isn't that obvious? As soon as the ice forms tonight you can all turn around and go back where you came from. All except you—you stay here for trial. And your son, if I recall correctly."

Marlowe held his temper. "That isn't what I mean. I want living space, with cooking and toilet accommodations, for five hundred people."

Beecher waved the problem away. "Let them stay where they are. A day won't hurt them. Teach them a lesson."

Marlowe started to answer, thought better of it and switched off. "You were right, Doc. There was no point in talking with him."

"Well—no harm done, either."

They went outside, there to find that Kelly had strung a line of his deputies around the scooters. "After you went

147

inside, Boss, I got uneasy, so I stationed some of the boys around."

"You're a better general than I am," Marlowe told him. "Any trouble?"

"One of Beecher's cops showed up, but he went away again."

"Why didn't you grab him?" asked MacRae.

"Well, I wanted to," Kelly answered, "but he kept going when I yelled at him. I couldn't stop him without shooting, so I let him go."

"Should have winged him," said MacRae.

"Should I have?" Kelly said to Marlowe. "I was tempted to, but I didn't know where we stood. Is this a shooting war, or is it just a row with the Company?"

"You did right," Marlowe assured him. "There will be no shooting unless Beecher starts it." MacRae snorted. Marlowe turned to him. "You disagree?"

"Jamie, you put me in mind of a case I ran into in the American West. A respected citizen shot a professional gun-thrower in the back. When asked why he didn't give the other chap a chance to draw, the survivor said, 'Well, he's dead and I'm alive and that's how I wanted it to be.' Jamie, if you use sportsmanship on a known scamp, you put yourself at a terrible disadvantage."

"Doctor, this is no time to swap stories. I've got to get these people safely housed and at once."

"That's my point," persisted MacRae. "Finding housing isn't the first thing to do."

"What is it, then?"

"Set up a task force of your best shots and send them over to grab Beecher and the Company offices. I volunteer to lead it."

Marlowe gestured angrily. "Out of the question. At present we are a group of citizens going about our lawful occasions. One move like that and we're outlaws."

MacRae shook his head. "You don't see the logic of the actions you've already taken. You know that water runs down hill, but you think it'll never reach the bottom. In Beecher's books you are an outlaw now. All of us."

"Nonsense, we're just enforcing our contract. If Beecher behaves, we'll behave."

"I'm telling you, son—the way to grasp a nettle is firmly."

"Doctor MacRae, if you are so sure how this matter should be conducted, why did you refuse to accept leadership?"

MacRae turned red. "I beg your pardon, sir. What are your orders?"

"You know Syrtis better than I do. Where is a building we can commandeer as a barracks?"

Jim decided that this was a good time to come out of hiding. "Dad," he said, coming around in front of him, "I know where we are and the school is—"

"Jim, I've no time to chat. Get in the car."

"But, Dad, it's only about ten minutes walk!"

"I think he's got something," put in the doctor. "The school will have real beds for the kids, and a kitchen."

"Hmmm . . . very well. Possibly we should use both schools and put the women and small children in the girls' school."

"Jamie," advised the doctor, "at the risk of getting my ears batted down again, I say 'no.' Don't divide your forces."

"I didn't really want to. Kelly!"

"Yes, sir."

"Get them all out and put a deputy in charge of each car party to keep them together. We're moving out."

"Right."

There is very little foot traffic in the streets of the Earth settlement at Syrtis Minor; pedestrians prefer to go by tunnel. The few they did meet seemed startled but no one bothered them.

The pressure lock at the school's front door could hold about twenty people at a time. As the outer door opened after the second load, Howe stepped out. Even with his mask on it could be seen that he was angry. "What is the meaning of this?" he demanded.

Willis took one look at him and closed up. Jim got behind his father. Marlowe stepped forward. "We're sorry but we've got to use the school as an emergency shelter."

"You can't do that. Who are you, anyway?"

"My name is Marlowe. I'm in charge of the migration."

"But—" Howe turned suddenly, pushed his way through the crowd and went inside.

Nearly thirty minutes later Marlowe, MacRae, and Kelly went inside with the last party. Marlowe directed Kelly to station guards on the inside at each door. MacRae considered suggesting a string of armed guards around the outside of the building, but he held his tongue.

Mr. Sutton was waiting for Marlowe in the entrance hall. "A news flash from Mrs. Palmer, Chief—she says to tell you that chow will be ready in about twenty minutes."

"Good! I could use a bite myself."

"And the school's regular cook is sulking in the dining room. She wants to talk to you."

"You deal with her. Where is Howe?"

"Derned if I know. He went through here like a destroying angel."

A man pressed forward—the entrance hall was jammed, not only with colonists but with students. Reunions were going on all around, between parents and sons. Kelly was pounding a smaller replica of himself on the back, and was himself being pounded. The babble was deafening. The man who had forced his way forward put his mouth to Marlowe's ear and said, "Mr. Howe is in his office. He's locked himself in; I've just come from trying to see him."

"Let him stay," decided Marlowe. "Who are you?"

"Jan van der Linden, instructor here in natural sciences. Who, may I ask, are you?"

"Name's Marlowe. I'm in charge of this mad house. Look here, could you round up the boys who live outside the school? We are going to have to stay here for a day or two at least. You might as well send the town boys home—and the teachers, too."

The teacher looked doubtful. "Mr. Howe won't like me doing it without his say-so."

"I'm going to do it in any case but you can speed things up. I take full responsibility."

Jim saw his mother through the crowd and did not wait

to hear the outcome. She was leaning against the wall, holding Oliver and looking very tired. Phyllis was standing close to her. Jim wormed his way through the crowd. "Mother!"

She looked up. "What is it, Jimmy?"

"You come with me."

"Oh, Jimmy—I'm too tired to move."

"Come on! I know a place where you can lie down." A few minutes later he had the three in the room abandoned by Frank and himself. His mother sank down on his bunk. "Jimmy, you're an angel."

"You take it easy. Phyl can bring you something to eat. I'm going back and see what's going on." He started to leave, then hesitated. "Phyl—would you take care of Willis for me?"

"Why? I want to see what's doing, too."

"You're a girl; you'd better stay out from under foot."

"Well, I like that! I guess I've got just as much business——"

"Stop it, children. Jimmy, we'll take care of Willis. Tell your father where we are."

Jim delivered the message, then found himself late in the chow line. By the time he had gone through for seconds, and eaten same, he discovered that most of the colonists were gathered in the school auditorium. He went in, spotted Frank and Doctor MacRae and squeezed over to them.

His father was pounding for order, using the butt of his gun as a gavel. "Mr. Linthicum has the floor."

The speaker was a man about thirty with an annoyingly aggressive manner. "I say Doctor MacRae is right, we shouldn't fool around. We've got to have boats to get to Copais. Right? Beecher won't give 'em to us. Right? Even if he deputizes every man in Syrtis he only has maybe a hundred and fifty guns. Right? We've got twice that many. Besides which Beecher won't be able to get all the local employees to fight us. So what do we do? We go over and grab him by the neck and force him to do right by us. Right?" He sat down triumphantly.

MacRae muttered, "Heaven defend me from my friends."

Several tried to speak; Marlowe picked one out. "Mr. Gibbs has the floor."

"Mr. Chairman . . . neighbors . . . I have rarely heard a more rash and provocative speech. You persuaded us, Mr. Marlowe, to embark on this reckless adventure, a project of which I never approved——"

"You came along!" someone shouted.

"Order!" called Marlowe. "Get to the point, Mr. Gibbs."

"—but in which I acceded rather than oppose the will of the majority. Now the hasty and ill-tempered would make matters worse with outright violence. But now that we are here, at the seat of government, the obvious thing to do is to petition for redress of grievances."

"If you mean by that to ask Beecher for transportation to Copais, Mr. Gibbs, I've already done so."

Gibbs smiled thinly. "Forgive me, Mr. Marlowe, if I say that the personality of the petitioner sometimes affects the outcome of the petition? I understand we have here, Mr. Howe, the Headmaster of this school and a person of influence with the Resident Agent General. Would it not be wise to seek his help in approaching the Resident?"

Mr. Sutton shouted, "He's the last man on Mars I'd let speak for me!"

"Address the chair, Pat," Marlowe cautioned. "I feel the same way, but I won't oppose it if that's what the crowd wants. But," he continued, to the audience, "is Howe still here? I haven't seen him."

Kelly stood up. "Oh, he's here; he's holed up in his office. I've talked to him through the ventilator. I've promised him a honey of a beating if he will only come out and stand up to me like a man."

Mr. Gibbs looked scandalized. "Well, really!"

"It's a personal matter involving my boy," explained Kelly.

Marlowe banged the table. "I imagine Mr. Kelly will waive his privilege if you folks want Howe to speak for you. Do I hear a motion?" Gibbs proposed it; in the end only he and the Pottles voted for it.

After the vote Jim said, "Dad?"

"Address the chair, son. What is it?"

"Er, Mr. Chairman—I got an idea. I was wondering, since we haven't got any boats, maybe we could get to Copais the way Frank and I got back to Charax—that is, if the Martians would help us." He added, "If folks wanted us to, I guess Frank and I could go back and find Gekko and see what could be done about it."

There was a moment of silence, then murmurs of "What's he talking about?" Although almost all of the colonists had heard the two boys' story, it was the simple fact that it had not been believed, or had been ignored or discounted. The report ran counter to experience and most of the colonists were as bogged down in "common sense" as their relatives back on Earth.

Mr. Marlowe frowned. "We don't know that the natives have these conveyances between here and Copais——"

"I'll bet they have!"

"—and we don't know that they would let us ride in them even if they have."

"But, Dad, Frank and I——"

"A point of order, Mr. Chairman!" It was Gibbs again. "Under what rules do you permit children to speak in the councils of adults?"

Mr. Marlowe looked embarrassed; Doctor MacRae spoke up. "Another point of order, Mr. Chairman. Since when does this cream puff—" He motioned at Gibbs.

"Order, Doctor."

"Correction. I mean this fine upstanding male citizen, Mr. Gibbs, get the notion that Frank and Jim and the other gun-toting men their age ain't citizens? I might add that I was a man grown when this Gibbs party was still drooling on his bib——"

"Order!"

"Sorry. I mean even before he had reached that stage. Now this is a frontier society and any man old enough to fight is a man and must be treated as such—and any girl old enough to cook and tend babies is adult, too. Whether you folks know it or not, you are headed into a period when you'll have to fight for your rights. The youngsters will do the fighting; it behooves you to treat them accordingly. Twenty-five may be the right age for citizenship in a moribund, age-ridden society back on Earth, but we aren't bound to follow customs that aren't appropriate to our needs here."

Mr. Marlowe banged his gun. "I declare this subject out of order. Jim, see me later. Has anyone any action to propose that can be carried out at this time? Do we negotiate, or do we resort to force?"

Mr. Konski said, "I favor taking what we have to have, if necessary, but it may not be necessary. Wouldn't it be well for you, Mr. Marlowe, to phone Mr. Beecher again? You could point out that we have force enough to do as we see fit; perhaps he will see reason. I so move."

The motion was carried; Mr. Marlowe suggested that someone else speak for them, but was turned down. He left the rostrum and went out to the communications booth. It was necessary to break the lock Howe had placed on it.

Beecher seemed pleased with himself. "Ah, yes—my good friend, Marlowe. You've called to give yourself up?"

Marlowe explained civilly to Beecher the purpose of his call.

"Boats to Copais?" Beecher laughed. "Scooters will be ready at nightfall to take the colonists back to South Colony. All who are ready to go at that time will escape the consequences of their hasty actions. Not you, of course."

"Let me point out to you that we are considerably larger in numbers than the largest force you can drum up here in Syrtis Minor. We intend to carry out the contract. If you crowd us into using force to get our rights, force we will use."

Beecher sneered through the TV screen. "Threats do not move me, Marlowe. Surrender. Come out one at a time and unarmed, hands up."

"Is that your last word?"

"One more thing. You are holding Mr. Howe a prisoner. Let him go at once, or I shall see to it that you are prosecuted for kidnapping."

"Howe? He's not a prisoner; he's free to leave at any time."

Beecher elaborated. Marlowe answered, "That's a private matter between Kelly and Howe. You can call Howe in his office and tell him so."

"You must give him safe conduct," Beecher insisted.

Marlowe shook his head. "I'm not going to interfere in a private quarrel. Howe is safe where he is; why should I bother? Beecher, I am offering you one more chance to provide boats peacefully."

Beecher stared at him and switched off.

Kelly said, "Maybe you should have thrown me to the wolves, Chief."

Marlowe scratched his chin. "I don't think so. I can't hold a hostage—but this building is safer with Howe in it. So far as I know there isn't a bomb nor any other heavy weapon in Syrtis—but I would like to know what makes Beecher so confident." ·

"He's bluffing."

"I wonder." Marlowe went back and reported the conversation to all the colonists.

Mrs. Pottle stood up. "Well, *we* are accepting Mr. Beecher's gracious offer at once! As for holding poor Mr. Howe a prisoner—why, the very idea! I hope that you are properly punished, and that ungentlemanly Mr. Kelly as well. Come, dear!" Again she made a grand exit, with Mr. Pottle trotting after.

Marlowe said, "Any more who want to surrender?"

Gibbs looked around uncertainly and followed them. No one spoke until he had left, then Toland said, "I move that we organize for action."

"Second!"—"Second the motion!"

No one wanted to debate it; it was carried. Toland then proposed that Marlowe be elected captain, with power to appoint officers. It, too, was carried.

At this point Gibbs came stumbling back, his face white, his hands trembling. "They're dead! They're dead!" he cried.

Marlowe found it impossible to restore order. Instead he crowded into the circle around Gibbs and demanded, "Who's dead? What happened?"

"The Pottles. I was almost killed myself." He quieted down enough to tell his story; the three had assumed their masks and gone out through the lock. Mrs. Pottle, without bothering to look around, had stomped out into the street, her husband a close shadow. As soon as they had stepped clear or the archway they had been both blasted. Their bodies lay in the street in front of the school. "It's your fault," Gibbs finished shrilly, looking at Marlowe. "You got us into this."

"Just a moment," said Marlowe, "did they do the things Beecher demanded? Hands up, one at a time, and so forth? Was Pottle wearing his gun?"

Gibbs shook his head and turned away. "That's not the point," MacRae said bitterly. "While we've been debating, Beecher has boxed us in."

XI

BESIEGED

IT WAS maddeningly true, as investigation soon proved. The front and back exits were covered by gunmen—Beecher's police, supposedly—who were able to blast anyone emerging from the building without themselves being under fire. The air-lock nature of the doors made a rush suicidal.

The school was at a distance from the settlement's dwellings; it was not connected by tunnel. Nor had it any windows. The colony listed hundreds of licensed gun wearers—and yet a handful of gun fighters outside could keep them holed up.

Under the influence of Doc MacRae's bellowing voice the assembly got back to work. "Before I go ahead," Marlowe announced, "does anyone else want to surrender? I'm fairly sure that the Pottles were shot because they blundered out without notice. If you shout and wave something white, I think your surrender will be accepted."

He waited. Presently a man got up with his wife, and

then another. A few more trickled out. They left in dead silence.

When they were gone Captain Marlowe went on with organizing. Mrs. Palmer he confirmed as head of commissary, Doc he designated as executive officer, Kelly he appointed officer of the watch, responsible for interior guard. Sutton and Toland were given the job of devising some sort of portable screen to block the enfilading fire that had dropped Mr. and Mrs. Pottle. Jim followed all this with excited interest until, after the appointment of platoon leaders, it became evident that his father did not intend to use boys as combatants. The students from the school were organized into two platoons, designated as reserve, and dismissed.

Jim hung around, trying to get a word with his father. At last he managed to catch his eye. "Dad——"

"Don't bother us now, Jim."

"But, Dad, you *told* me to see you about getting the Martians to help us get to Copais."

"The Martians? Oh—" Mr. Marlowe thought about it, then said, "Forget it, Jim. Until we can break out of here, neither that scheme, nor any other, will work. Go see how your mother is doing."

Thus brushed off, Jim turned disconsolately away. As he was leaving Frank fell in step with him. "Do you know, Jim, sometimes you aren't as full of guff as you are other times."

Jim eyed him suspiciously. "If that's a compliment—thanks."

"Not a compliment, Jim, merely justice. Seldom as I approve of your weary notions, this time I admit that you had a bright idea."

"Quit making a speech and get to the point."

"Very well. Point: when you suggested getting the Martians to help us you were firing on all jets."

"Huh? Well, thanks, but I don't see it myself. As Dad pointed out, there's nothing we can do about it until we find some way to break out of here. Then I suppose we won't need their help."

"You're supposing too fast. Let's as Doc would say, analyze the situation. In the first place, your father got us boxed in here——"

"You lay off my father!"

"I wasn't picking on your father. Your father is a swell guy. But by behaving like a gentleman he got us cornered and we can't get out. I'm not blaming him, but that's the situation. So what are they going to do about it? Your old man tells my old man and that drip Toland to work out a shield, some sort of armor, that will let us get out the door and into the open where we can fight. Do you think they'll have any luck?"

"Well, I hadn't thought about it."

"I have. They are going to get exactly no place. Dad is a good engineer. You give him equipment and materials and he'll build you anything. But what's he got to work with? He's got the school workshop and you know what a sad mess that is. The Company never spent any money on equipping it; it's about right for making book ends. Materials? What are they going to make a shield out of? Dining room table tops? A heater would cut through a table top like soft cheese."

"Oh, there must be something around they can use."

"You name it."

"Well, what do you want us to do?" Jim said in exasperation. "Surrender?"

"Certainly not. The old folks are stuck in a rut. Here's where we show finesse—using your idea."

"Quit calling it my idea. I haven't got any idea."

"Okay, I'll take all the credit. We get word to Gekko that we need help. He's our water friend; he'll see to it."

"How can Gekko help us? Martians don't fight."

"That's right, but, as it says in geometry, what's the corollary? Human beings never fight Martians, *never*. Beecher can't risk offending the Martians. Everybody knows what a terrible time the Company had persuading the Martians that it was all right to let us settle here in the first place. Now suppose that about twenty or thirty Martians—or even one—came stomping up to the front door of this place: what do Beecher's cops do?"

"Huh?"

"They cease fire, that's what—and we come swarming out. That's what Gekko can do for us. He can fix it so that Beecher is forced to call off his gun toters. He'll *have* to."

Jim thought about it. There was certainly merit in it. Every human who set foot on Mars had it thoroughly drummed into him that the natives must not be interfered with, provoked, nor their customs violated—nor, above all things, hurt. The strange and distressing history of the first generation of contact with the Martians had resulted in this being the first law of the settlements on Mars. Jim could not imagine Beecher violating this rule—nor could he imagine the Company police doing so. In normal times the principal duty of the police was the enforcement of this rule, particularly with respect to tourists from Earth, who were never allowed to come in contact with natives.

"There is just one thing wrong, Frank. Supposing Gekko and his friends were willing, how are we going to let him know that we need help? We can't just call him on the phone."

"No, we can't—but that is where you come in. *You* can send him a message."

"How?"

"Willis."

"You're crazy!"

"Am I? Suppose you go out that front door—*fsst!* You are done for. But suppose Willis goes out? Who's going to shoot a bouncer?"

"I don't like it. Willis might get hurt."

"If we just sit tight and do nothing, you'll wish he was dead. Beecher will sell him to the London Zoo."

Jim considered this, then answered, "Anyhow, your scheme is full of holes. Even if he gets outside safely, Willis couldn't find Gekko and couldn't be depended on to deliver a message. He'd be just as likely to sing or recite some of Doc's bum jokes. I've got a better idea."

"Convince me."

"I'll bet that Beecher's plug-uglies didn't think to keep

watch on the garbage dump. I'll deliver the message to Gek-ko myself."

Frank thought it over. "No good. Even if they aren't watching the dump, they can see you from where they are watching the back door. They'd nail you before you could scramble to your feet."

"I'll wait till dark."

"Mmmm . . . could work. Only I'll do it. I'm faster on my feet than you are."

"Look who's talking!"

"All right! We'll *both* do it—an hour apart." Frank went on, "But that doesn't cut Willis out of it. He'll try it, too. One of us might get through. Now wait a minute—you underrate your little pal. We'll teach him just what he's to say. Then you tell him to go over into the native city, stop the first Martian he meets and recite his piece. The Martian does the rest because we'll put it all into the message. The only question is whether or not Willis is bright enough to do as you tell him. I've got grave doubts about that."

Jim bristled. "You're always trying to make out that Willis is stupid. He's not; you just don't understand him."

"Okay, then he can find his way over to the city and deliver the message. Or can't he?"

"Well—I don't like it."

"Which do you prefer, to take a small risk with Willis or to have your mother and your baby brother have to spend the winter at South Colony?"

Jim chewed his lip. "All right—we'll try it. Let's get Willis."

"Don't get in a rush. Neither you nor I know the native language well enough to whip up just what we want to say. But Doc does. He'll help us."

"He's the only one of the grown ups I'd trust with this anyhow. Come on."

They found MacRae, but were not able to speak with him at once. He was in the communications booth, bellowing at the screen. They could hear his half of the conversation. "I want to talk to Doctor Rawlings. Well, get him—don't sit there chewing your pencil! Tell him it's Doctor MacRae. . . . Ah, good day, Doctor! . . . No, I just got here. . . .

How's business, Doctor? Still cremating your mistakes? . . . Well, don't we all? . . . Sorry, I can't; I'm locked up. . . . Locked up, I said . . .—L . . . O . . . C . . . K . . . E . . . D up, like a disorderly drunk. . . . No reason, none at all. It's that simian moron, Beecher. . . . Yes, hadn't you heard? The entire colony, penned up in the schoolhouse . . . shoots us down if we so much as stick our noses out. . . . No, I'm not joking. You know Skinny Pottle—he and his wife were killed not two hours ago. Come see for yourself and find out what kind of a madman you have ruling you here . . ." The screen suddenly went blank. MacRae swore and fiddled with the controls.

Presently, by experiment, he realized the instrument had been cut off completely. He came out, shrugging. "Well, they finally caught on to me," he remarked to the room in general, "but I talked to three key men."

"What were you doing, Doc?" asked Jim.

"Starting some fifth column activity behind Beecher's lines. There are good people everywhere, son, but you have to spell it out for them."

"Oh. Look, Doc, could you spare us some time?"

"What for? Your father has a number of things for me to do, Jim."

"This is important." They got MacRae aside and explained to him their plans.

MacRae looked thoughtful. "It just might work. That notion of making use of Martian immunity is brilliant, Frank; you should go into politics. However, about the other stunt— the garbage can paratrooper act—if you ask your father, he'll veto it."

"Can't you ask him? He'll listen to you"

"I said 'If you ask your father'."

"Oh. I get you."

"About the other matter—chase up the little beastie and meet me in the classroom 'C'; I'm using it as an office."

Jim and Frank left to do so. Jim found his mother and Oliver asleep, his sister and Willis gone. He had started to leave when his mother woke up. "Jimmy?"

"I didn't mean to wake you, Mother. Where's Phyl? I want to find Willis."

"Your sister is in the kitchen, I think, helping out. Isn't Willis here? He was here on the bed with baby and me."

Jim looked again, but found no sign of Willis. "I'll go ask Phyl. Maybe she came back and got him."

"He can't have wandered far. I'm sorry, Jim."

"I'll find him."

He went to the kitchen, found his sister. "How would I know?" she protested. "He was with mother when I left. Don't go looking at me."

Jim joined Frank. "Darn it, they've let him wander off. We'll just have to search."

One hour and hundreds of inquiries later they were convinced that, if the bouncer was in the school, he had found a very special hiding place. Jim was so annoyed that he had forgotten completely the essential danger that they were all in. "That's what comes of trusting women," he said bitterly. "Frank, what'll I do now?"

"Search me."

They were in the far end of the building from their former room. They started back toward it on the chance that Willis might have come back. As they were passing through the entrance hall, Jim stopped suddenly. "I heard him!"

They both listened. "Open up!" came a replica of Jim's voice. "Let Willis in!" The voice came through the door's announcing speaker.

Jim darted for the pressure lock, was stopped by the guard. "Hey," he protested, "open the lock. That's Willis."

"More likely it's a trap. Stand back."

"Let him in. That's Willis, I tell you." The guard ignored him, but threw the switch that caused the lock to cycle. He cleared everybody out of range, then watched the door from one side, gun drawn.

The inner door opened and Willis waddled through.

Willis was bland about the whole thing. "Jim go away. Everybody go away. Willis go for walk."

"How did you get outdoors?"

"Went out."

"But how?" Willis apparently could see nothing difficult about that; he did not amplify.

"Maybe he went out when the Pottles did?" suggested Frank.

"Maybe. Well, I guess it doesn't matter."

"Go see people," Willis offered. He named off a string of native names, then added, "Fine time. Water friends. Give Willis good water, big drink." He made lipsmacking noises in imitation of Jim, although he had no lips himself.

"You had a drink just a week ago," Jim said accusingly.

"Willis good boy!" Willis countered.

"Wait a minute," said Frank. "He was with *Martians*."

"Huh? I don't care if he was with Cleopatra; he shouldn't run away."

"But don't you see? He can get to the natives; he already has. All we've got to do is to be sure he carries a message for them to pass on to Gekko."

The point, relayed to MacRae, increased his interest. The three composed a message in English for MacRae to translate. "Greetings," it began, "this is a message from Jim Marlowe, water friend of Gekko of the city of—" Here they inserted the unspellable and almost unpronounceable Martian name of Cynia. "Whoever you may be, friend of my friend, you are implored to send this word at once to Gekko. I am in great trouble and I need your help." The message went on to tell the nature of the trouble, who was responsible, and what they hoped would be done about it. Telegraphic simplicity was not attempted, since Willis's nervous sysem could hold a thousand words as easily as ten.

MacRae translated it, then drilled Jim in reading it, after which they attempted to impress on Willis what he was to do. Willis was willing, but his consistently slap-happy, featherbrained approach to any problem exasperated them almost to hysteria. At last it seemed likely that he might carry out his assignment; at least (a) when asked what he was to do he would answer, "go see friends," and (b) when asked what he would tell them he would (usually) answer by reciting the message.

"It might work," decided MacRae. "We know the Martians have means of rapid communication, even though we've never known what sort. If our plump friend doesn't forget what he is doing and why he is making the trip . . ."

Jim took him to the front door. On MacRae's authorization the guard let them through. Jim checked Willis again while the lock was cycling; the bouncer appeared to be sure of his instructions, although his answers showed his usual mental leapfrog.

Jim hung back in the doorway, out of the line of fire, while Willis rolled off the stoop. The Pottles still lay where they had fallen; Willis looked at them, then took a zig-zag course down the street and disappeared from Jim's view, cut off as he was by the door frame. Jim wished then that he had had the foresight to bring along a mirror to use as a periscope. Finally he screwed up his courage, lay down, and peeked around the edge of the door at the bottom-most part.

Willis was well down the street and nothing had happened to him. Far down the street some sort of a cover had been set up. Jim stuck his head out an inch farther trying to see what it was, when the corner of the door frame above him gave off a puff of smoke and he felt the electric tingle of a near miss. He jerked his head back and re-entered the lock.

He had an all-gone feeling at the pit of his stomach and a conviction that he would never see Willis again.

XII

"DON'T SHOOT!"

THE DAY passed wearily for Jim and Frank. There was nothing they could do about their own plan until after dark. In the meantime discussions were taking place among colonial leaders, but they were held behind closed doors and the boys were not invited.

Supper was welcome diversion, both because they were hungry and because it meant that the kitchen would presently be deserted and the way left open to the garbage dump. Or so they thought. They found that, in practice, the womenfolk running the kitchen first took a leisurely time to clean up, then seemed disposed to sit around all night, drinking coffee and talking.

The boys found excuses to come into the kitchen, excuses which began to arouse Mrs. Palmer's suspicions. Finally Jim followed another boy in, wondering what he would say this time, when he heard the other boy say, "Mrs. Palmer, Captain Marlowe wants to know if it would be too much trouble to keep a night watch for coffee and sandwiches for the men on guard."

"Why, no," Jim heard her say, "we'll be glad to. Henrietta, will you find some volunteers? I'll take the first stint."

Jim backed out and went to where Frank awaited him. "What's the chances?" asked Frank. "Does it look like they're going to break up any time soon?"

Jim told him what the chances were—or, rather, were not. Frank swore, using a couple of words that Jim had not heard before. "What'll we do, Jim?"

"I don't know. Maybe when it's down to just one of them, she'll go out occasionally."

"Maybe we could get her out with some song and dance."

"Maybe we could tell her that she's wanted in the headquarters room. That ought to do it."

They were still discussing it when the lights went out.

The place was suddenly as dark as the inside of a rock. Worse than that, there was a disturbing silence. Jim had just realized that the complete emptiness of sound resulted from the ending of the noise of circulating air, from the stopping of the supercharger on the roof, when a woman began to scream.

She was joined by another, in a higher key. Then there were voices everywhere in the darkness, questioning, complaining, soothing.

Down the hall a light sprang out and Jim heard his father's voice. "Quiet, everybody. It's just a power failure. Be patient."

The light moved toward them, suddenly hit them. "You boys get to bed." Jim's father moved on. In the other direction they could hear Doc's bellow, ordering people to shut up and calm down.

Jim's father came back. This time he was saying, "Into your suits, everybody. Have your respirators on your head. We hope to correct this in a few minutes, but we don't want anybody hurt. Don't get excited; this building will hold pressure for half an hour at least. Plenty of time to get ready for thin air, even if it takes a while to correct the trouble."

Other lights sprang up; shortly the passageways throughout the building, if not the rooms, were adequately lighted. The corridors were crowded with dim shapes, struggling into their outdoors suits. Jim and Frank, planning as they were to attempt to go outside, had long been in their suits, armed, and with respirators at the ready. "Maybe this is a good time," suggested Frank.

"No," Jim answered. "They're still in the kitchen. I can see a light."

MacRae came down the corridor; Jim stopped him. "Doc,

how long do you think it will be until they get the lights on?"

MacRae said, "Are you kidding?"

"What do you mean, Doc?"

"This is one of Beecher's stunts. He's pulled the switch on us, at the power house."

"Are you sure?"

"There's no failure—we've checked it. I'm surprised Beecher didn't do it hours ago. But don't you birds go blabbing, Jim; your Pop has his hands full keeping the nervous nellies from blowing their tops." He moved on.

In spite of Captain Marlowe's reassuring words the true state of things was soon common knowledge. The pressure dropped slowly, so slowly that it was necessary to warn everyone to adjust his respirator, lest oxygen starvation sneak up on the unwary. After that it was hardly possible to maintain the fiction that the power loss was temporary, to be corrected any minute now. The temperature in the building fell slowly; there was no danger of them freezing in the closed and insulated building—but the night chill penetrated.

Marlowe set up headquarters in the entrance hall in a circle of light cast by a single torch. Jim and Frank loitered there, discreetly back in the shadows, unwilling to miss what might be going on and quite unwilling to go to bed as ordered . . . as Frank pointed out to Jim, the only beds they had were occupied, by Mrs. Marlowe, Phyllis, and Oliver. Neither of them had given up the idea of attempting the garbage chute route, but they knew in their hearts that the place was too stirred up to give them the privacy they would require.

Joseph Hartley, one of the colony's hydroponists, came up to Marlowe. His wife was behind him, carrying their baby daughter in a pressurized crib, its supercharger sticking up above the clear plastic shell of it like a chimney. "Mr. Marlowe—I mean Captain Marlowe——"

"Yes?"

"You've got to do something. Our kid can't stand this. She's coming down with croup and we can't get at her to help her."

MacRae crowded forward. "You should have brought her to me, Joe." He looked the baby over, through the plastic, then announced, "The kid seems to be doing all right."

"She's sick, I tell you."

"Hmm—I can't make much of an examination when I can't get at her. Can't take her temperature, but she doesn't seem to be in any real danger."

"You're just trying to soothe me down," Hartley said angrily. "You can't tell anything about it when she is in a sealed crib."

"Sorry, son," the doctor answered.

"A lot of good it does to be sorry! Somebody's got to *do* something. This can't—" His wife plucked at his sleeve; he turned away and they went into a huddle. Shortly he turned back. "Captain Marlowe!"

"Yes, Mr. Hartley."

"The rest of you can do as you like. I've had enough. I've got my wife and baby to think about."

"The decision is yours," Marlowe said stiffly and turned away in abrupt dismissal.

"But—" said Hartley and stopped, aware that Marlowe was no longer paying any attention to him. He looked uncertain, like a man who wants someone to argue him out of his resolution. His wife touched his arm; he turned then and they went together to the front entrance.

Marlowe said to MacRae, "What do they expect of me? Miracles?"

MacRae answered, "Exactly, boy. Most people never grow up. They expect papa to get 'em the pretty Moon." The doctor went on, "Just the same, Joe accidentally told the truth. We've got to do something."

"I don't see what we can do until Sutton and Toland get some results."

"You can't wait any longer for them, son. We've got to crush out of here anyway. Theoretically a man can live for days in a respirator. Practically, it won't work and that is what Beecher is counting on. You can't keep several hundred people crouching here in the dark and the cold, wearing masks to stay alive, not indefinitely. You're going to have a panic on your hands."

Marlowe looked weary, even through his mask. "We can't tunnel out. We can't get out at all, except through the doors. And they've got those doors zeroed. It's suicide."

"It's got to be done, son. I'll lead the rush."

Marlowe sighed. "No, I will."

"You've got a wife and kids. I've got nobody and I've been living on borrowed time so long I've lost track."

"It's my privilege. That settles it."

"We'll see."

"I said that settles it, sir!"

The argument was left unfinished; the inner door to the pressure lock opened again and Mrs. Hartley stumbled inside. She was clutching the tiny crib and sobbing wildly.

It was the case of the Pottles and Gibbs all over again. When MacRae was able to make something out of her sobs, it appeared that they had been very cautious, had waited, had shouted their intention to surrender, and had displayed a light. There had been no answer, so they had shouted again, then Hartley had stepped off the threshold with his hands up and his wife shining the light on him.

He had been struck down as soon as he stepped out the door.

MacRae turned her over to the women, then went out to reconnoiter. He came back in almost at once. "Somebody get me a chair," he demanded, and looked around. "You, Jim—skedaddle."

"What's up?" asked Marlowe.

"Let you know in a moment. I suspect something."

"Be careful."

"That's why I want the chair."

Jim came back with one; the doctor went through the pressure lock again. He came back in about five minutes later. "It's a booby trap," he stated.

"What do you mean?"

"Beecher didn't try to keep men outdoors all night—at least I don't think so. It's automatic. They've put an electric-eye grid across the door. When you break it, a bolt comes across, right where you'd be if you walked through it." He displayed half a dozen deep burns through the chair.

Marlowe examined them. "But that's not the important point," MacRae went on. "It's automatic but it's inflexible. It hits about two feet above the step and about four feet. A man could crawl through it—if his nerves were steady."

Marlowe straightened up. "Show me."

They came back, with the chair still more burned, in a few minutes. "Kelly," Marlowe said briskly, "I want twenty volunteers to make a sortie. Pass the word around."

There were at least two hundred volunteers. The problem was to weed them down. Both Frank and Jim tried to get in on it. Jim's father refused to take any but grown, unmarried men—except himself. MacRae he refused.

The doctor pulled Jim back and whispered to him. "Hold your horses. In a few minutes I'll be boss."

The raiding party started into the lock. Marlowe turned to MacRae. "We'll head for the power plant. If we are gone more than two hours, you are on your own." He went into the lock and closed the door.

As soon as the door was closed, MacRae said, "Okay, twenty more volunteers."

Kelly said, "Aren't you going to wait two hours?"

"You tend to your knitting! When I'm out of here, you're in charge." He turned and nodded to Jim and Frank. "You two come along." MacRae had his party in short order, had apparently selected them in his mind before Marlowe left. They filed into the lock.

Once the outer door was open MacRae flashed his torch into the street. The Pottles and the unfortunate Joseph Hartley lay where they had fallen, but no other bodies littered the street. MacRae turned around and said, "Gimme that chair. I'll demonstrate the gimmick." He stuck it out into the door. Instantly two bolts cut across the doorway, parallel to the ground. After they were gone and the eye was still dazzled by their brilliance, two soft violet paths of ionization marked where they had been and then gradually dispersed.

"You will note," said the doctor, as if he were lecturing medical students, "that it does not matter where the chair is inserted." He again shoved the chair into the opening, moved it up and down. The bolts repeated at split-second intervals, but always at the same places, about knee high and chest high.

"I think it is best," continued the doctor, "to maintain the attack. Then you can see where you are. First man!"

Jim gulped and stepped forward—or was shoved, he was not sure which. He eyed the deadly fence, stooped over, and with awkward and infinite care stepped through. He went on out into the street. "Get moving!" the doctor ordered. "Spread out."

Jim ran up the street, feeling very much alone but terribly excited. He paused short of the end of the building and cautiously looked around the corner. Nothing either way—he stopped and waited in the darkness, ready to blast anything that moved.

Ahead of him and to the left he could see the curious structure which had almost cost him the top of his head many hours before. It was clear now that the bolts were coming from it.

Someone came up behind him. He whirled and heard a voice yelp, "Don't shoot! It's me—Frank."

"How about the others?"

"They're coming—I think."

A light flashed at the building ahead, beyond the shield from which the bolts came. Frank said, "I think somebody came out there."

"Can you see him? Do you think we ought to shoot?"

"I don't know."

Someone else was pounding up the street behind them. Up ahead, from near the spot where Frank had thought he had seen a man a heater flashed out in the darkness; the beam passed them.

Jim's gun answered by pure reflex; he nailed the spot from which the flash had come. "You got him," said Frank. "Good boy!"

"I did?" said Jim. "How about the guy behind me?" He found that he was trembling.

"Here he is now."

"Who shot at me?" the newcomer said. "Where are they?"

"Nowhere at the moment," Frank answered. "Jim nailed him." Frank tried to peer into the mask; the night was too dark. "Who is it?"

"Smitty."

Both Frank and Jim gave exclamations of surprise—it was Smythe, the practical man. "Don't look at me like that," Smythe said defensively. "I came along at the last minute— to protect my investment. You guys owe me money."

"I think Jim just paid it off," suggested Frank.

"Not on your life! That's another matter entirely."

"Later, later," said Frank. Others were coming up. Presently MacRae came puffing up and roared, "I told you bird brains to spread out!" He caught his breath and said, "We tackle the Company main offices. Dogtrot—and don't bunch together."

"Doc," said Jim, "there are some in that building up ahead."

"Some what?"

"Somebody that shoots at us, that's what."

"Oh. Hold it, everybody." MacRae gave them hoarse instructions, then said, "Got it, everybody?"

"Doc," asked Frank, "how about the gun over there? Why don't we wreck it first?"

"I must be getting old," said MacRae. "Anybody here enough of a technician to sneak up on it and pull its teeth?"

A faceless figure in the darkness volunteered. "Go ahead," Doc told him. "We'll cover you from here." The colonial trotted ahead, swung around behind the shield covering the stationary automatic blaster, and stopped. He worked away for several minutes, then there was a white flash, intensely bright. He trotted back. "Shorted it out. Bet I blew every overload breaker in the power house."

"Sure you fixed it?"

"You couldn't dot an 'i' with it now."

"Okay. You—" MacRae grabbed one of his squad by the arm. "—tear back and tell Kelly. You—" He indicated the chap who had wrecked the gun. "—go around in back and see what you can do with the set up back there. You two guys cover him. The rest of you follow me—the building ahead, according to plan."

Jim's assignment called for sneaking along the face of the building and taking a covering position about twenty feet short of the doorway. His way led him over the ground where the man had been at whom he had shot. There was no body on the pavement; he wondered if he had missed. It was too dark to look for blood.

MacRae gave his covering troops time to reach their stations, then made a frontal assault with six to back him up, among them Frank. The doctor himself walked up to the building entrance, tried the outer door. It opened. Motioning the assault group to join him, he went in. The outer door of the building's lock closed on them.

Jim huddled against the icy wall, eyes wide, ready to shoot. It seemed a cold eternity that he waited; he began to fancy that he could see some traces of dawn in the east. At last he saw silhouettes ahead, raised his gun, then identified one as Doc's portly figure.

MacRae had the situation in hand. There were four disarmed prisoners; one was being half carried by two others. "Take 'em back to the school," Doc ordered one of his group. "Shoot the first one of them who makes a funny move. And tell whoever is in charge back there now to lock 'em up. Come on, men. We've got our real job ahead."

There came a shout behind them; MacRae turned. Kelly's voice called, "Doc! *Wait for us!*" He came running up and demanded, "What are the plans?" Behind him, men were pouring out of the school and up the street.

MacRae took a few minutes to recast things on the basis of more guns. One of the platoon leaders, a civil engineer named Alvarez, was left in charge at the school with orders to maintain a guard outside the building and to patrol the neighborhood with scouts. Kelly was assigned the task of capturing the communications building which lay between the settlement and the space port. It was an important key to control of the whole situation, since it housed not only the local telephone exchange but also the radio link to Deimos and thence to all other outposts on Mars—and also the radar beacons and other aids for incoming ships from Earth.

MacRae reserved for himself the job of taking the planet office—the main offices on Mars of the Company, Beecher's own headquarters. The Resident Agent General's personal apartment was part of the same building; the doctor expected to come to grips with Beecher himself.

MacRae sent a squad of men to reinforce Marlowe at the power house, then called out, "Let's go, before we all freeze to death. Chop, chop!" He led the way at a ponderous trot.

Jim located Frank in the group and joined him. "What took you guys so long in that building?" he asked. "Was there a fight?"

"Took so long?" said Frank. "We weren't inside two minutes."

"But you must have——"

"Cut out that chatter back there!" called out Doc. Jim shut up and pondered it.

MacRae had them cross the main canal on ice, avoiding the arching bridge as a possible trap. They crossed in pairs, those behind covering those crossing; in turn they who had crossed spread out and covered those yet to come. The crossing held a nightmarish, slow-motion quality; while on the ice a man was a perfect target—yet it was impossible to hurry. Jim longed for his skates.

On the far side the doctor gathered them together in the shadow of a warehouse. "We'll swing around to the east and avoid the dwellings," he told them in a hoarse whisper. "From here on, *quiet!*—for your life. We won't split up because I don't want you shooting each other in the dark." He set forth a plan to surround the building and cover all exits, while MacRae himself and about half their numbers tried to force an entrance at the main door.

"When you get around in back and make contact," Mac-Rae warned the two who were to lead the flanking and covering moves, "you may have one deuce of a time telling friend from foe. Be careful. The word is 'Mars'; the answer is 'Freedom'."

Jim was in the assault party. Doc stationed six of them in fan shape around the door, at an easy twenty-five yards range, and had them take cover where available. Three of them were on the open ramp in front of the door; he had them lie down and steady their guns. "In case of doubt—shoot," he instructed them. "Come on, the rest of you."

Jim was included in the last order. MacRae walked up to the outer door and tried it; it was locked. He pressed the signal switch and waited.

Nothing happened. MacRae pressed the switch again and called out mildly to the speaker grille, "Let me in. I have an important message for the Resident."

Still nothing happened. MacRae changed his tone to pretended exasperation. "Hurry up, please! I'm freezing to death out here."

The door remained dark and silent. MacRae changed his manner to belligerence. "Okay, Beecher, open up! We've got the place surrounded and we're ready to blast in the door. You have thirty seconds till we set off the charge."

The seconds ticked away. Doc muttered to Jim, "I wish it were the truth," then raised his voice and said, "Time's up, Beecher. This is it."

The door hissed as the compressed air in the lock began to escape to the outside; the lock was starting to cycle. MacRae motioned them back a little; they waited, not breathing, all guns drawn and aimed at the point where the door would begin to open.

Then it was open and a single figure stood in it, the lock's light shining behind him. "Don't shoot!" said a firm, pleasant voice. "It's all right. It's all over."

MacRae peered at the figure. "Why, Doctor Rawlings!" he said. "Bless your ugly face."

XIII

"IT'S AN ULTIMATUM"

RAWLINGS HIMSELF had spent half the night locked up, along with half a dozen other prominent citizens who had attempted to reason with Beecher. As the story got around, especially the matter of the deaths of the Pottles, Beecher found himself with no support at all, save from his own clique of sycophants and toadies and the professional, largely disinterested support of the Company's police.

Even Kruger cracked up under 'the strain, tried to get Beecher to reverse himself—and was stuffed in with the others, which by then included the chief engineer of the power plant. But it was Doctor Rawlings who talked the guard placed over them into risking his job and letting them go—the doctor was treating the guard's wife.

"I don't think Beecher would ever stand trial, even if we had him back on Earth," MacRae remarked about the matter to Rawlings and Marlowe. "What do you think, Doctor?" The three were seated in the outer offices of the planet office building. Marlowe had come there after getting word at the power house from MacRae and had gotten busy at once, writing despatches to the Project camps and the other outlying activities, including North Colony itself, trying to round up boats. He had then tried, red-eyed and uncertain from lack of sleep, to compose a suitable report to Earth, until MacRae had interrupted him and insisted that he get some rest first.

"Paranoia?" said Rawlings.

"A clear case."

"My opinion, too. I've seen suggestive indications of it, but the case was not fully developed until his will was crossed. He must be hospitalized—and restrained." Dr. Rawlings glanced over his shoulder at a closed door. Behind it was Beecher.

Rawlings turned back. "What do you think of Howe, Doctor?"

MacRae grunted. "Haven't seen enough of him to have an opinion. What do you plan to do with him, Jim?" he added, turning to Marlowe.

Marlowe frowned. "Nothing. The only charges we can make stick aren't worth the trouble. We'll simply ship him back."

MacRae nodded. "That's the ticket. Hanging's too good for him; kick him out."

"What worries me more," Marlowe went on, "is whom to get to replace him. The school has to be running again before we leave for Copais. Why don't you volunteer to fill in, Doc? Temporarily, of course."

MacRae stared. "Me? Heaven forbid!"

"Well, I've got to have somebody to ride herd on those youngsters, somebody who can do it without using a strait-jacket. They all like you."

"No—repeat—emphatically—no!"

"There is a young fellow already with the school," volunteered Rawlings, "whom Professor Steuben was grooming for the job when the Company sent Howe instead. Chap named van der Linden. Seems a good, sensible sort. My boy likes him."

Marlowe looked interested. "I ran into him. He was helpful. Of course I don't have any real authority to appoint him."

MacRae snorted. "Jamie, you'll be the death of me!"

Marlowe put down his coffee cup and wiped his mouth. "All that is as may be. I think I'll stretch out on one of these desks for a couple of hours. Doc, will you see that someone wakes me?"

"Certainly," agreed MacRae, having no intention of allowing the man to be disturbed until he was fully rested. "Don't worry."

Jim and the others were back at the school where they were to remain until boats could be gotten to take them to Copais. Mrs. Palmer was bustling around with her assistants, getting a mammoth breakfast for weary men and boys. Jim himself was dead tired and hungry but much too excited to think about sleeping, even though dawn had broken outside.

He had just received a cup of coffee and was blowing on it when Smythe showed up. "Say, I understand you really did kill that cop that took a pot shot at me."

"No," Jim denied, "he's in the infirmary now, just wounded. I've seen him."

Smythe looked troubled. "Oh, shucks," he said finally, "it won't happen more than once in a lifetime. Here's your I.O.U."

Jim stared at him. "Smitty, you're sick."

"Probably. Better take it."

Jim reached back into his subconscious memory and quoted his father. "No, thanks. Marlowes pay their debts."

Smythe looked at him, then said, "Oh, the heck with you, you ungracious twerp!" He tore the I.O.U. into small pieces and stalked away.

Jim looked wonderingly after him. "Now what was he sore about?" He decided to look up Frank and tell him about it.

He found Frank but had no time to tell him about it; a shout came through the crowd: "Marlowe! Jim Marlowe!"

"Captain Marlowe's at the planet office," someone answered.

"Not him, the kid," the first voice replied. "Jimmy Marlowe! You're wanted up front, right away."

"Coming," yelled Jim. "What for?" He pushed his way toward the entrance, Frank behind him.

The man who had paged him let him get close before he answered, "You won't believe it—I don't myself. Martians."

Jim and Frank hurried outside. Gathered in front of the school door were more than a dozen Martians. Gekko was there, and G'kuro, but not K'boomch. Nor could Jim make out the old one whom he thought of as "head man" of

Gekko's tribe. Gekko spotted them and said in his own speech, "Greetings, Jim-Marlowe, greetings, Frank-Sutton, friends sealed with water."

Another voice called out from one of Gekko's palm flaps, "Hi, Jim boy!" Willis had come home with the bacon, a little late perhaps, but successfully.

Another voice boomed mellowly. Gekko listened, then said, "Where is he who stole our little one?"

Jim, uncertain of the dominant tongue, at best, was not sure that he had understood. "Huh?"

"He wants to know where Howe is," said Frank and answered in fluent, fairly accurate Martian. Howe was still where he had taken refuge, still afraid to face Kelly, despite repeated invitations.

Gekko indicated that he would come into the building. Amazed, but co-operative, the boys led him in. Gekko was forced to fold himself into a shape resembling a hat rack to get into the lock but he managed it; the lock was large. Inside, the sensation caused by his appearance was like that which might have resulted from introducing an elephant into a church. People gave way before him.

The door to the outer office was even more of a squeeze than the air lock, but Gekko made it, with Jim and Frank trailing him. Gekko handed Willis to Jim, then gently explored the handle of the door to Howe's office with a hand flap. Suddenly he pulled and the door came away, not only the lock broken but the door wrenched completely off its hinges. He squatted down further, completely filling the door frame.

The boys looked at each other; Willis closed up. They heard Howe saying "What's the meaning of this? Who are——"

Then Gekko stood up as well as he could in a room intended for humans and started for the outer door. The boys hesitated; Frank said, "Let's see what he did to him." He stepped to the wrecked door and looked in. "I don't see him. Hey, Jim—he's not in here at all."

Nor was he.

They hurried after Gekko and reached him at the air

lock. No one stopped Gekko; no one stopped them. The repeated indoctrination concerning Martians swept a path before them. Outside Gekko turned to them. "Where is the other one, who would do harm to the little one?"

Frank explained that Beecher was some distance away and not available. "You will show us," announced Gekko and picked them both up. Another Martian relieved him of Frank.

Jim felt himself cradled in the soft palm flaps, even as Willis was still cradled in Jim's arms. Willis extended his eyes, looked around and remarked, "Fine ride, huh?" Jim was not sure.

The Martians ambled through town at an easy eight miles an hour, over the bridge, and to the planet offices. The pressure lock there was higher and larger than that at the school; the entire party went inside. The ceiling of the building's foyer was quite high enough for even the tallest Martian. Once they were inside Gekko set Jim down, as did the Martian carrying Frank.

There had been the same scurrying surprise as at the school. MacRae came out and looked the situation over without excitement. "What's all this jamboree?" he asked.

"They want to talk to Beecher," Frank explained.

MacRae raised his eyebrows, then spoke in clear Martian. One of them answered him; they conversed back and forth. "Okay, I'll get him," agreed MacRae, then repeated it in Martian. He went into the offices. He returned in a few minutes, pushing Beecher in front of him, and followed by Rawlings and Marlowe. "Some people to see you," Mac-Rae said and gave Beecher a shove that carried him out onto the floor of the foyer.

"This is the one?" inquired the Martian spokesman.

"This is verily the one."

Beecher looked up at them. "What do you want me for?" he said in Basic. The Martians moved so that they were on all sides of him. "Now you get away from me!" he said. They moved in slowly, tightening the circle. Beecher attempted to break out of it; a great hand flap was placed in his way. They closed in further. Beecher darted this way and that, then he was concealed completely from the spectators by a screen of palm flaps. "Let me out!" he was heard to shout. "I didn't do anything. You've got no right to—" His voice stopped in a scream.

The circle relaxed and broke up. There was no one inside it, not even a spot of blood on the floor.

The Martians headed for the door. Gekko stopped and said to Jim, "Would you return with us, my friend?"

"No—oh, no," said Jim. "I have to stay here," then remembered to translate.

"And the little one?"

"Willis stays with me. That's right, isn't it, Willis?"

"Sure, Jim boy."

"Then tell Gekko so." Willis complied. Gekko said farewell sadly to the boys and to Willis and went on out the lock.

MacRae and Rawlings were in whispered, worried conference at the spot where Beecher had last been seen; Captain Marlowe was looking sleepy and confused and listening to them. Frank said, "Let's get out of here, Jim."

"Right."

The Martians were still outside. Gekko saw them as they came out, spoke to one of his kind, then said, "Where is the learned one who speaks our speech? We would talk with him."

"I guess they want Doc," said Frank.

"Is that what he meant?"

"I think so. We'll call him." They went back inside and dug MacRae out of a cluster of excited humans. "Doc," said Frank, "they want to talk with you—the Martians."

"Eh?" said MacRae. "Why me?"

"I don't know."

The doctor turned to Marlowe. "How about it, Skipper? Do you want to sit in on this?"

Mr. Marlowe rubbed his forehead. "No, I'm too confused to try to handle the language. You take it."

"Okay." MacRae went for his suit and mask, let the boys help dress him, and then did not deny them when they tagged along. However, once outside, they held back and watched from a distance.

MacRae walked down to the group standing on the ramp and addressed them. Voices boomed back at him. He entered the group and the boys could see him talking, answering, gesticulating with his hands. The conference continued quite a long time.

Finally MacRae dropped his arms to his sides and looked tired. Martian voices boomed in what was plainly farewell, then the whole party set out at a rapid, leisurely pace for the bridge and their own city. MacRae plodded back up the ramp.

In the lock Jim demanded, "What was it all about, Doc?"

"Eh? Hold your peace, son."

Inside MacRae took Marlowe's arm and led him toward the office they had pre-empted. "You, too, Rawlings. The rest of you get about your business." Nevertheless the boys tagged along and MacRae let them come in. "You might as well hear it; you're in it up to your ears. Mind that door, Jim. Don't let anyone open it."

"Now what is it?" asked Jim's father. "What are you looking so grim about?"

"They want us to leave."

"Leave?"

"Get off Mars, go away, go back to Earth."

"What? Why do they suggest that?"

"It's not a suggestion; it's an order, an ultimatum. They aren't even anxious to give us time enough to get ships here from Earth. They want us to leave, every man jack, woman, and child; they want us to leave right away—and they aren't fooling!"

XIV

WILLIS

FOUR DAYS LATER Doctor MacRae stumbled into the same office. Marlowe still looked tired, but this time it was MacRae who looked exhausted. "Get these other people out of here, Skipper."

Marlowe dismissed them and closed the door. "Well?"

"You got my message?"

"Yes."

"Is the Proclamation of Autonomy written? Did the folks go for it?"

"Yes, it's written—we cribbed a good deal from the American Declaration of Independence I'm afraid, but we wrote one."

"I'm not interested in the rhetoric of the thing! How about it?"

"It's ratified. Easily enough here. We had quite a few startled queries from the Project camps, but it was accepted. I guess we owe Beecher a vote of thanks on that; he made independence seem like a fine idea."

"We owe Beecher nothing! He nearly got us all killed."

"Just how do you mean that?"

"I'll tell you—but I want to know about the Declaration. I had to make some promises. It's gone off?"

"Radioed to Chicago last night. Too soon to expect an answer. But let me ask the questions: were you successful?"

"Yes." MacRae rubbed his eyes wearily. "We can stay. 'It was a great fight, Maw, but I won.' They'll let us stay."

Marlowe got up and started to set up a wire recorder. "Do you want to talk it into the record and save having to go over it again?"

MacRae waved it away. "No. Whatever formal report I make will have to be very carefully edited. I'll try to tell you about it first." He paused and looked thoughtful. "Jamie, how long has it been since men first landed on Mars? More than fifty Earth years, isn't it? I believe I have learned more about Martians in the past few hours than was learned in all that time. And yet I don't know anything about them. We kept trying to think of them as human, trying to force them into our molds. But they aren't human; they aren't anything like us at all."

He added, "They had interplanetary flight millions of years back . . . had it and gave it up."

"*What?*" said Marlowe.

"It doesn't matter. It's not important. It's just one of the things I happened to find out while I was talking with the old one, the same old one with whom Jim talked. By the way, Jim was seeing things; he's not a Martian at all."

"Wait a minute—what is he, then?"

"Oh, I guess he's a native of Mars all right, but he isn't what you and I mean by a Martian. At least he didn't look like one to me."

"What did he look like? Describe him."

MacRae looked puzzled. "Uh, I *can't*. Maybe Jim and I each saw what he wanted us to see. Never mind. Willis has to go back to the Martians and rather soon."

"I'm sorry," Marlowe answered. "Jim won't like that, but it's not a high price to pay if it pleases them."

"You don't understand, you don't understand at all. Willis is the key to the whole thing."

"Certainly he's been mixed up in it," agreed Marlowe, "but why the key?"

MacRae rubbed his temples. "It's very complicated and I don't know where to start. Willis *is* important. Look, Jamie, you'll go down in history as the father of your country, no doubt, but, between ourselves, Jim should be credited for Willis's love for Jim and Jim's staunch befriending of him—

that the colonists are alive today instead of pushing up daisies. The ultimatum to get off this globe represented a concession made to Jim; they had intended to exterminate us."

Marlowe's mouth dropped open. "But that's impossible! Martians wouldn't do anything like that!"

"Could and would," MacRae stated flatly. "They've been having doubts about us for a long time. Beecher's notion of shipping Willis off to a zoo pushed them over the edge—but Jim's relationship to Willis pulled them back again. They compromised."

"I can't believe that they would," protested Marlowe, "nor can I see how they could."

"*Where's Beecher?*" MacRae said bluntly.

"Mmm . . . yes."

"So don't talk about what they can or can't do. We don't know anything about them . . . not *any*thing."

"I can't argue with you. But can you clear up some of this mystery about Jim and Willis? Why do they care? After all, Willis is just a bouncer."

"I don't think I can clear it up," MacRae admitted, "but I can sure lace it around with some theories. Do you know Willis's Martian name? Do you know what it means?"

"I didn't know he had one——"

"It reads: 'In whom the hopes of a world are joined.' That suggest anything to you?"

"Gracious, no!"

"I may have translated it badly. Maybe it means 'Young Hopeful,' or merely 'Hope.' Maybe Martians go in for poetical meanings, like we do. Take my name, 'Donald.' Means 'World Ruler.' My parents sure muffed that one. Or maybe Martians enjoy giving bouncers fancy names. I once knew a Pekinese called, believe it or not, 'Grand Champion Manchu Prince of Belvedere'." MacRae looked suddenly startled. "Do you know, I just remembered that dog's family-and-fireside name was Willis!"

"You don't say!"

"I do say." The doctor scratched the stubble on his chin and reflected that he should shave one of these weeks. "But it's not even a coincidence. I suggested the name 'Willis' to Jim in the first place; I was probably thinking of the Peke. Engaging little devil, with a pop-eyed way of looking at you just like Willis—our Willis. Which is to say that neither one of Willis's names necessarily means anything."

He sat so long without saying anything that Marlowe said, "You aren't clearing up the mystery very fast. You think that Willis's real name does mean something, don't you?—else you wouldn't have brought it up."

MacRae sat up with a jerk. "I do. I do indeed. I think Willis's name is meant literally. Now wait a minute—don't throw anything. I won't get violent. What do *you* think Willis is?"

"Me?" said Marlowe. "I think he's an example of exotic Martian *fauna*, semi-intelligent and adapted to his environment."

"Big words," complained the doctor. "*I* think he is what a Martian is before he grows up."

Marlowe looked pained. "There is no similarity of structure. They're as different as chalk and cheese."

"Granted. What's the similarity between a caterpillar and a butterfly?"

Marlowe opened his mouth and closed it. "I don't blame you," MacRae went on, "we never think of such metamorphosis in connection with higher types, whatever a 'higher type' is. But I think that is what Willis is and it appears to be why Willis has to go back to his people soon. He's in the nymph stage; he's about to go into a pupal stage—some sort of a long hibernation. When he comes out he'll be a Martian."

Marlowe chewed his lip. "There's nothing unreasonable about it—just startling."

"Everything about Mars is startling. But if my theory is correct—and mind you, I'm not saying it is—then it might explain *why* Willis is such an important personage. Eh?"

Marlowe said wearily, "You ask me to assimilate too much at once."

"Emulate the Red Queen. I'm not through. I think the Martians have still another stage, the stage of the 'old one' to whom I talked—and I think it's the strangest one of all.

Jamie, can you imagine a people having close and everyday relations with Heaven—*their* heaven—as close and matter of fact as the relations between, say, the United States and Canada?"

"Doc, I'll imagine anything you tell me to."

"We speak of the Martian 'other world'; what does it mean to you?"

"Nothing. Some sort of a trance, such as the East Indians indulge in."

"I ask you because I talked, so they told me, to someone in the 'other world'—the 'old one' I mean. Jamie, I think I negotiated our new colonizing treaty with a *ghost*.

"Now just keep your seat," MacRae went on. "I'll tell you why. I was getting nowhere with him so I changed the subject. We were talking Basic, by the way; he had picked Jim's brains. He knew every word that Jim might know and none that Jim couldn't be expected to know. I asked him to assume, for the sake of argument, that we were to be allowed to stay—in which case, would the Martians let us use their subway system to get to Copais? I rode one of those subways to the conference. Very clever—the acceleration is always *down*, as if the room were mounted on gymbals. The old one had trouble understanding what I wanted. Then he showed me a globe of Mars—very natural, except that it had no canals. Gekko was with me, just as he was with Jim. The old one and Gekko had a discussion, the gist of which was *what year was I at?* Then the globe changed before my eyes, bit by bit. I saw the canals crawl across the face of Mars. *I saw them being built,* Jamie.

"Now I ask you," he concluded, "what kind of a being is it that has trouble remembering which millennium he is in? Do you mind if I tag him a ghost?"

"I don't mind anything," Marlowe assured him. "Maybe we're all ghosts."

"I've given you one theory, Jamie; here is another: bouncers and Martians and Old Ones are entirely separate races. Bouncers are third class citizens, Martians are second class citizens, and the real owners we never see, because they live down underneath. They don't care what we do with the surface as long as we behave ourselves. We can use the park, we can even walk on the grass, but we mustn't frighten the birds. Or maybe the 'old one' was just hypnosis that Gekko used on me, maybe it's bouncers and Martians only. You name it."

"I can't," said Marlowe. "I'm satisfied that you managed to negotiate an agreement that permits us to stay on Mars. I suppose it will be years before we understand the Martians."

"You are putting it mildly, Jamie. The white man was still studying the American Indian, trying to find out what makes him tick, five hundred years after Columbus—and the Indian and the European are both *men*, like as two peas. These are *Martians*. We'll never understand them; we aren't even headed in the same direction."

MacRae stood up. "I want to get a bath and some sleep ... after I see Jim."

"Just a minute. Doc, do you think we'll have any real trouble making this autonomy declaration stick?"

"It's got to stick. Relations with the Martians are eight times as delicate as we thought they were; absentee ownership isn't practical. Imagine trying to settle issues like this one by taking a vote back on Earth among board members that have never even *seen* a Martian."

"That's not what I mean. How much opposition will we run into?"

MacRae scratched his chin again. "Men have had to fight for their liberties before, Jamie. I don't know. It's up to us to convince the folks back on Earth that autonomy is necessary. With the food and population problem back on Earth being what it is, they'll do anything necessary—once they realize what we're up against—to keep the peace and continue migration. They don't want anything to hold up the Project."

"I hope you're right."

"In the long run I have to be right. We've got the Martians pitching on our team. Well, I'm on my way to break the news to Jim."

"He's not going to like it," said Jim's father.

"He'll get over it. Probably he'll find another bouncer and teach him English and call him Willis, too. Then he'll grow up and not make pets of bouncers. It won't matter." He looked thoughtful, and added, "But what becomes of Willis? I wish I knew."

ROBERT A. HEINLEIN